Murdering the Roses

A Heavenly Highland Inn Cozy Mystery

Cindy Bell

ISBN-13: 978-1492919605

ISBN-10: 1492919608

More Cozy Mysteries by Cindy Bell

Hairspray and Homicide (Bekki the Beautician Cozy Mystery 1)

A Dyed Blonde and a Dead Body (Bekki the Beautician Cozy Mystery 2)

Mascara and Murder (Bekki the Beautician Cozy Mystery 3)

Pageant and Poison (Bekki the Beautician Cozy Mystery 4)

.

Table of Contents

Chapter One

The blood curdling scream that carried through the grand old inn was enough to draw the attention of every living creature with the ability to hear in the nearby area. The Heavenly Highland Inn was fairly isolated from the rest of the small town where it was located, but there were plenty of wild animals in the woods that surrounded it that went scampering for cover. Vicky looked up sharply from all of the swatches and brochures that were spread out across her desk that she was reviewing. The bride to be that had booked the upcoming weekend wedding at the inn had some very specific requests. But as she heard the commotion, her stomach tightened with fear as she recognized the scream as belonging to her Aunt Ida.

Vicky jumped up from her desk and raced out of the small office in her apartment. Vicky's shoulder length, dark brown hair bounced as she moved so fast. Her deep green eyes were wide with fear and uncertainty as she wondered what could be happening that was so horrible. She ran out into the hallway of the main floor of the inn, following the sound of the shrieking. The inn was three stories with guest rooms on each floor, aside from the main floor, which only housed Vicky's apartment, the lobby, the kitchen and the lounge. When she reached the bottom of the stairs that led up to Aunt Ida's room, her older sister, Sarah, joined her.

"What is it?" she asked. She looked just as panicked as Vicky felt. The two women were five years apart in age but at that moment they felt like two little girls about to find a monster under the bed.

"I don't know!" Vicky frowned. "But we need to find out." The wail came again and both women rushed up the sprawling staircase to the second floor. Sarah and Vicky were both rather tall and slender, but Sarah had their mother's wavy, blonde hair and dark brown eyes, while Vicky's looks took more after her father. The inn was very old, and had retained its original character despite many attempts at renovating and redecorating it. It was as if it had its own personality and memories. Even the wooden railing, that Vicky slid her palm along to keep her balance as she moved quickly, had the same nicks and grooves that she could remember inspecting as a child. She didn't have to think about it, she had them memorized. Hours spent running up and down the stairs, just for the fun of it, before her mother would insist that she stop because her running back and forth was making her dizzy. The inn had been the sisters' playground as children, and now it was their last remaining connection to their parents.

"Aunt Ida?" Vicky shouted as they neared the door to her room. Aunt Ida lived in one of the guest rooms in the inn, but most of the time she was out wandering around, spying on the guests or snooping on Vicky to see what she was up to. If she wasn't spying or snooping, then she was in the lounge, flirting with every man she could find. When Vicky tried to turn the knob on the door, it wouldn't budge. But Aunt Ida was still screaming.

"Aunt Ida?" Vicky called out again and banged on the door so hard that the wooden surface shook. Sarah pushed her gently aside and withdrew the set of keys she kept on her at all times. As the manager of the inn she took her job very seriously. She was always watching out for the guests and making sure that everyone was taken care of. It came naturally to her as she was a mother of two rambunctious boys, and knew how to multi-task for the sake of her sanity. When she unlocked the door, Vicky braced herself for what she might find inside. Was there an ax murderer? Was Aunt Ida dangling from one of the outside windows?

She pushed past her sister and into the room, expecting to find the worst case scenario. However, she didn't find anything at all, except for Aunt Ida's collection of outlandish furniture that clashed with absolutely everything anyone could imagine. She had a red leather couch paired with a plush black recliner that eased onto an oriental rug. Aunt Ida's strange fashion sense really made the eyes hurt when someone first looked at it. But Aunt Ida was not on the couch or in the recliner. Her screams were coming from the bathroom.

"Vicky, is that you?" Aunt Ida called out in a trembling voice. "Vicky please help me! It is absolutely horrifying!"

Vicky was not one to ever deny her aunt aid so she opened the door to the bathroom, while Sarah peered curiously over her shoulder. They were both used to their aunt's overly dramatic antics, but neither really knew what to expect.

They looked towards the tub, and there they saw something that neither really wanted to see, their aunt, with the shower curtain wrapped around her, standing in the bath tub.

"Are you hurt?" Vicky asked with confusion, she didn't see any blood or obvious injury. Had the shower curtain somehow attacked Aunt Ida? Maybe she had watched a scary movie.

"I can't get out," Ida huffed, her screams finally ceasing now that she saw that both of her nieces had come to her aid. "I'm so glad you're here, I thought I would be stuck in this tub for days if no one heard me screaming." She shook her head, water dripping from her short hair.

"Why were you screaming?" Sarah asked in an even tone as she tried to keep her frustration at bay. She was trying to figure out just what was going on here. Aunt Ida was a very important person to the sisters. Four years before, their parents had been killed in a tragic car accident. It was so sudden and so heartbreaking to lose both parents on the same day. Sarah had a young child and a young marriage, and Vicky had just graduated from college. Both were in transitional stages of their lives and were not prepared to be left with no guiding force or support from the parents they adored. Aunt Ida, who had lived in the inn even when her sister and brother-in-law were alive, had stepped in as a motherly figure after the sisters decided to split the responsibilities of running the famous get away for the rich. Since then she had been a part of their daily lives, and she really did make an effort to show them how much she cared for them. She also managed to make an effort to be very dramatic at least once a day.

"Well, obviously because of that," Ida pointed across from her at the bathroom mirror, her extended finger shaking. At first all that Vicky saw was the steam from the shower that had caused the mirror to fog. Then she noticed something rather massive curled around the edge of the mirror.

"A spider!" Sarah gasped out with irritation. "That's what all of that screaming was about?" She looked absolutely enraged as she stalked over to her aunt with a towel. "Really, it's not like this isn't an old building, spiders are going to get in now and then."

Vicky shifted uncomfortably from foot to foot as she stared at the large brown and hairy creature that seemed to be staring right back at her.

"Well, it is very big," Vicky said in a trembling voice. She was not afraid of many things, but massive spiders watching her take a shower just might make the list.

"Humongous!" Aunt Ida squeaked out as she nervously took the towel from Sarah and wrapped it around her. Aunt Ida was a very beautiful woman, despite her age. She was older than her sister who had passed, and in her late sixties she could easily pass for much younger. She took very good care of herself and always had some new beauty treatment or lotion for Vicky to try. They shared a love of décor and fashion, even if it didn't always match. Where Vicky preferred things to be a bit more subtle Aunt Ida had a preference for the outlandish, as was demonstrated by her taste in furniture, and her abnormal reaction to a spider that surely couldn't have caused her too much harm if she had just stepped out of the shower.

"Get rid of that thing," Sarah muttered to Vicky as she escorted Aunt Ida out of the bathroom to help her settle down.

"Me?" Vicky gasped, her eyes wide as she

shook her head firmly at her sister. "I'm not going near that thing!" she insisted.

"Someone has to get rid of it!" Sarah called back with clear annoyance. "It's not going to be me," she added. "Maybe I can get Phil to come take care of it," she said thoughtfully. Phil was her husband, and though he was rather straight laced and far too traditional for Vicky's taste she had to admit that if Sarah asked him to he would probably drop everything at work and come right over to take care of the spider. He had been a strong source of comfort for Sarah when their parents passed, and even Vicky had leaned on him a few times for some stability and the promise that things would eventually get better.

"What's going on here, I heard screaming?" a voice said from the doorway of the room, which had been left ajar in their panic to save their aunt from whatever horrible assailant was attacking her. It was Bob, the newest hire at the inn. Bob and Vicky knew each other from high school. They hadn't really known each other well, just attended the same grade at the same time. But when she was growing up she knew his mother quite well as she was involved in Vicky's volleyball team. So when Bob came to Vicky looking for any kind of work he could get his hands on, she had decided to take a chance on him.

It was a decision she had made out of sympathy and something she had regretted ever since. He was lazy, not very good at his job, and always sneaking drinks from the lounge. Henry, the chef for the inn had already come to her three times, livid that the fresh vegetables he was supposed to serve straight from the garden, were wilted or rotten. Sarah had insisted that Vicky needed to get rid of Bob, since she was the one who had hired him, but Vicky just couldn't bring herself to do it. No matter how bad an employee he was, he was still a person. She hated to think of him living without any kind of income, as she had been his last resort for a job. She kept hoping that he would simply start doing better and she could drop the whole idea of firing him.

Bob wasn't a looker either. He had scars on his face from past acne, and his skin was dark from working in the sun for so long, but instead of looking tanned, it just looked dirty. His hair was always greasy as if he didn't shower very often, and the scent he carried pretty much proved that theory time and time again. It was no different today as Sarah shielded their aunt from his presence, considering she was still only in a towel. However, for the first time since Vicky had hired him, she was happy to see him.

"Bob we need you to do something for us," Vicky said quickly. While Sarah was shielding Aunt Ida, Vicky led him into the bathroom and showed him the massive intruder.

"Would you look at that," Bob clucked his tongue with admiration. "I've seen a few of these in the garden shed, but none this big," he reached up as if he might grab the spider with his bare hand.

"Ugh! Use something, like a towel, or toilet paper, or at least a cup," Vicky pleaded, her stomach churning at the very idea of those long, hairy legs scraping against skin. He laughed a little and snatched up a paper towel from the counter. The paper towel looked fairly small in comparison to the size of the spider.

"This should do it," he said quietly as he reached for the spider again. He seemed to be fascinated, rather than frightened by it.

"Wait!" Vicky squealed in terror as he was about to grab it. "Wait until I get out of the room!" What if it escaped and chased after her?

"Okay, okay," he grinned with a devilish glint in his eyes. Vicky wondered if he was considering throwing that arachnid beast at her. She hurried out of the bathroom and climbed up onto her Aunt Ida's bed. Sarah rolled her eyes, but when they heard Bob give a shout from the bathroom, Sarah also pulled her feet up onto the bed, with a grimace.

"Got it!" Bob finally said as he came out with the balled up paper towel. He held it up in the air triumphantly.

"Is it in there?" Aunt Ida asked, her eyes huge with fear.

"Sure, want to see it?" Bob offered and held the paper towel out to the cluster of women.

"No!" Aunt Ida shrieked and waved her hand wildly in Bob's direction. "Go get rid of that thing! Put it out of its misery!"

Bob began to leave the room laughing and shaking his head as he did. Vicky tried to regain her composure after feeling so flustered.

"Aunt Ida, you really shouldn't have been screaming like that," Vicky said sternly. "We thought you were in serious danger."

"I was," Aunt Ida argued. "Didn't you see the size of that thing?"

"That's not serious danger," Sarah said sharply, though her irritation was softened by an affectionate chuckle. "Serious danger is when someone is coming at you with a knife, not when you are being faced with a spider that may or may not have even gone near you. With all that screaming I'm surprised the thing didn't run away and hide from you."

"Me too," Vicky agreed with a laugh.

"That's why I was so scared," Ida pointed out with a sigh. "It wasn't behaving in a frightened way. If I had stepped out of that shower, that sucker would have launched itself right at me, I know it!"

All three laughed a little at the idea of the spider attacking. Now that it was gone it seemed like something that could be laughed about.

"Well, we have work to do," Sarah said with a sigh, as so far the morning had been a doozy. "Are you going to be okay by yourself?" she asked.

"Of course I will, now that thing is gone," Ida said with a shudder. "Thank you, for coming to my rescue girls."

Sarah and Vicky couldn't help but smile fondly at their aunt.

"Anytime," Vicky assured her as she stood up from the bed. Sarah leaned over to pick up one of the pillows that had been knocked onto the floor, and caught sight of something as Bob was stepping out of the room. Sarah nodded her head towards Vicky, and pointed to the tattoo that his rolled up sleeve had exposed. Vicky jumped up and followed after him, her anger building as she approached him.

"Bob!" she said sharply, and he spun swiftly around to face her.

"What?" he asked, still holding the paper towel carefully in his hand.

"I asked you to make sure that you covered that tattoo," she reminded him. The tattoo was of a snake wrapped around a blade. She didn't personally have a problem with it other than that she thought it was rather ugly, but their discerning customers expected a certain level of professional decorum.

"Oh sorry," he muttered and gave a slight shrug. "I'll try to remember."

"Please do," Vicky said sternly as she looked at him. "We deal with very high end clients and I don't want them seeing you walking around the grounds with that tattoo showing, or they might think that you're some kind of criminal."

Bob smirked slightly. It was just a glimmer of an expression, but enough to make Vicky wonder if she had done a thorough enough background check on him.

"Sure thing, boss," he called back over his shoulder and used his free hand to tug the sleeve of his shirt down to his wrist. Sarah soon joined her in the hallway.

"Did you fire him?" she asked hopefully.

"Of course not," Vicky said with a frown. "He just rescued us from a giant spider, it didn't feel like the right time."

"When is going to be the right time?" Sarah frowned, her expression growing impatient. "When he has finished murdering the roses?"

Vicky sighed and nodded. Bob did not have any kind of a green thumb and since his arrival the extensive gardens on the large property had been much worse for it. She couldn't think of anyone she had ever known that had a worse way with plants. Yet, she still felt if she gave him a little more time that maybe he could straighten himself out. He didn't have anyone to turn to, as his mother had passed and his brother was estranged. His father was useless, and always had been, he had never shown an ounce of affection to his boys or wife. Vicky felt so lucky in comparison to him. She had a stable life and so many people that cared about her, so she had been sympathetic enough to give him a chance. The question was, how long that sympathy was going to last. Was it going to last long enough to allow him to destroy their gardens! The gardens were one of the big draws of the inn. That along with the amazing mountain views that overlooked the most lush scenery in the area.

Wealthy people from different countries all around the world would seek out the inn when they were visiting the United States. People would reserve their weddings two years in advance to ensure that they would have the chance to get married in such a beautiful place. It really was a gem nestled in the middle of wide open nature. Her parents had bought it on a lark when they were young. It was a deal that her father had been unable to pass up, even though he knew it would be a lot for him to handle. But they had done it, working together, while at the same time raising two young girls.

Vicky didn't know anyone else who had the chance to grow up amidst such beauty and history, so she really did consider herself lucky. At least she had, until the tragic accident had stolen her parents from her. After that she had felt a little more cautious about the world around her. Things no longer seemed so gentle or non-threatening.

Chapter Two

"Have you seen Mitchell today?" Sarah asked, attempting to disguise her nosiness as casual curiosity.

"No, why would I?" Vicky replied, gritting her teeth. She had had one date with the deputy sheriff, and Aunt Ida and Sarah had been on top of her about it ever since. Vicky liked Mitchell just fine, but she was gun shy about relationships. It wasn't that she had ever been scarred, it was that she wasn't sure she was ready to share her life with anyone else. Watching the way Sarah and Phil were together could be very beautiful at times, but sometimes it seemed very limiting. Sarah and Phil didn't often argue, but they did give up a lot in order to maintain their marriage, raise their children, and keep the inn afloat. It all seemed as if it might be a little too much of a struggle than it was worth. Vicky figured if the time was right she would know it. For now, Mitchell was a good companion and she was interested in getting to know him better, but she wasn't in any rush.

As she stepped out of the elevator with her

sister beside her, she checked her phone. It didn't seem to her that Mitchell was interested in rushing things either, considering she hadn't heard from him in three days. Vicky wondered if her feisty personality had frightened the homegrown deputy sheriff. Maybe her excursions into college life and the wild times she recounted to him had made him think twice about whether Vicky was the down-to-earth woman he was looking for. Or it could have been the fact that she had ordered a double dessert.

Vicky was always herself, whether the person she was with liked it or not. Her thoughts were distracted by a striking gentleman who was waiting at the counter to be checked in. Sarah walked over to the counter and began to set him up with a room. Vicky overheard him volunteering to pay in cash, and leave a generous security deposit to cover any potential damages. It was not unusual to have well off clients at the inn but it was a little strange to have them pay in cash. As the man walked away Vicky wandered over to her sister.

"What was that about?" she asked with interest, it had been a while since they had such a handsome young guest.

"His name is Timothy," Sarah said in a hushed tone, her eyes wide with intrigue. "I think he must be trying to hide out from the press, or maybe even on the run, because he didn't even want to give me his last name! He paid for everything in cash," she tapped a few keys on the keyboard as she spoke.

"You don't think he's dangerous, do you?" Vicky asked with a frown as she studied the man who was heading for the elevator.

"No, I don't think so. He's probably one of those celebrities that gets hounded everywhere he goes, that, or maybe he is just trying to evade his wife or mistress," she pointed out with a distasteful grimace.

"I think you've been reading too many romance novels," Vicky giggled and Sarah shot her a glare.

"There's nothing wrong with believing in a little romance Vicky. Maybe you should try it some time," she arched a brow knowingly. It was a bone of contention between the sisters that Vicky was so casual about being single, while Sarah seemed convinced that her sister needed to be more open to being swept off her feet.

"Ha ha," Vicky stuck out her tongue at her sister.

"Don't you have some romantic weddings to work on?" Sarah reminded her with a mischievous smile as she turned back to the list of guests she was reviewing.

"Yes, actually, I do," Vicky nodded and walked off towards the banquet hall. The banquet hall was huge and took up one half of the inn. It had a ballroom dance floor that could be converted into just about anything to satisfy their guests. They had once even created an indoor ice skating rink for a woman who wanted a winter wedding in the middle of July. It really had been a beautiful ceremony, Vicky had to admit. Not exactly her taste, but amazing just the same. There was something very special about being the driving force behind someone having their fantasy wedding come true.

As she settled down with the information for the latest wedding she thought about the gardens. She really was going to have to do something before Bob destroyed them. The inn had a lot to offer but the gardens were a big part of its allure especially for spring weddings. The blooms were in every shade imaginable and were huge, and with full and normally unbruised petals.

As her mind drifted through the plans and requests that the current bride had made for her wedding on the following weekend, Vicky's mind slipped into an imaginative world. She had a knack for visualizing things, and then bringing them to life. She could see the trail of rose petals that the woman wanted to walk across, as well as hear the violins that she wanted to have playing. The ceremony would be perfect, Vicky would make sure of it. She might not believe so strongly in romance, but she did believe that anything could be accomplished with the right amount of focus and determination.

As she was in this peaceful state she was suddenly disrupted by what sounded like two men arguing. She stood up from the table and listened more closely. The flying insults seemed to be coming from the kitchen which was attached to the banquet hall. She frowned and walked towards the kitchen to see what the argument was about. That was another thing that neither she nor Sarah tolerated around guests. It was important that those who paid such high dollars to stay there were treated to an escape from their daily lives not an immersion in conflict between employees. When she stepped into the kitchen she found Henry, the head chef, and Bob going head to head. Both men looked so angry that they might be ready to deliver blows.

"What's going on in here?" Vicky demanded as she looked between the two of them incredulously. Henry had worked for them for years, and she had never seen him so riled up. Bob on the other hand, she recalled, had a temper even in high school.

"Why don't you ask Bob?" Henry said sharply as he turned back towards the counter. "Ask him why I have to put up with visits and phone calls from his brother!" Vicky sighed as she realized that this was yet another consequence of her choice to hire Bob.

"Why is that?" Vicky asked as she looked towards Bob. "Are you in some kind of trouble?"

"No," Bob said with a deepening frown. "I just owe him a little bit of money, and I've been trying to duck him. But this genius told him I work here," Bob growled at Henry as if the entire situation was his fault.

"Listen, how was I supposed to know that you

would steal from your own family?" Henry hissed back. "I mean I knew that you were pathetic, but I didn't know that you would sink that low," his eyes were flashing with fury as he slung his insults.

Henry had pulled Vicky aside a few times to warn her about Bob. He had told Vicky time and time again not to trust the man, as he felt that Bob was hiding something. Vicky had attempted to defend Bob, but all of Henry's warnings were turning out to be true.

"Listen, I don't want you bringing any of this trouble here," Vicky said sharply as she glared at Bob. "You should have told me about this before I hired you Bob! I can't have family members stalking our employees."

"If I had told you, then you wouldn't have hired me, and I need the money Vicky," he whined with such an annoying tone that Vicky had to look away to keep from glaring more fiercely. She was very tempted to fire him right then, but Vicky was not an impulsive person. She liked to think things through before taking action.

"Well, no matter the reason, if he comes here

again, I'm going to have to take action," Vicky warned. "I don't want any of my employees to be harassed."

"I'm sorry," Bob said with a sigh and scratched at the back of his neck. "I'll make sure he stays away, I promise."

"You do that," Henry snapped with annoyance at Bob.

Bob looked as if he might punch Henry right in the nose, which Vicky couldn't let happen, as who would cook the fancy meals for their customers then? She stepped between the two of them.

"Enough," she said sharply. "You're both trying my patience. Now break it up. I don't want to see the two of you anywhere near each other anymore, understand?"

Both men nodded reluctantly and Bob stepped out through the kitchen door and into the garden that backed up to the staff's quarters behind the inn. It was a simple building but still very beautiful and gave the staff plenty of room to live in.

"Henry, are you okay?" Vicky asked as she looked over at the man. He was a bit older than

Bob, in his forties, and he had a great reputation for being an amazing chef. So far Vicky had never heard a single complaint about his food. She didn't want to lose him over a bad gardener.

"Yes I'm fine," Henry sighed and turned back to the pot of sauce he had been stirring. "But you really shouldn't let riff raff like that work here, it brings down the morale!"

Vicky frowned as she was once again reminded that it was her mistake in the first place that had brought Bob on as a member of staff. She spent the rest of the day finishing the final preparations for the wedding coming up on the weekend, and listing over and over in her mind just why she needed to fire Bob. It amazed her that he could be so different from his mother, who had been a kind and warm person who always made an effort to be there for those she knew. That was why she had tried to help Bob out.

When she finished with all she could do that day for the wedding she went off in search of Sarah. They always said goodbye to each other each night before Sarah would head home to the house she shared with her husband and two sons. The boys would sometimes come to the inn to play. When they did it reminded Vicky so much of growing up together with Sarah in the inn. It could really be a fun and interesting place to spend your childhood. As she walked up the stairs to the second floor in search of her sister she noticed Timothy standing in the hallway. He didn't seem to be heading in any particular direction, he was just wandering.

"Hello there," Vicky smiled at him in a friendly manner. "Is there anything I can help you with?'

When his eyes settled on Vicky there was nothing friendly about them. In fact they were extremely cold to the point that it made Vicky's skin crawl.

"No thanks, just checking the place out," he finally said, his tone as cold as his eyes.

"All right, well if you need anything at all please feel free to ask," she smiled again, hoping to gain some kind of warmth in response from him. But he only nodded and continued to walk past her. Vicky turned and watched him walk away, still feeling a little puzzled about his behavior. Didn't he have anything better to do than wander around the inn?

Vicky found Sarah speaking to one of the maids at the end of the second floor.

"I just want to make sure that all the rooms are prepared for our guests this weekend, so if we need to give the week night maids some overtime to get that done, then just let me know," Sarah was explaining to Martha. Martha was white-haired and in her seventies. She was in charge of the maids and had just about as much say about what happened in the inn as Vicky and Sarah did. She wasn't an owner, but she had been there longer than the two of them had been alive, so they gave her respect where respect was due.

"I think the day staff should be able to handle it," Martha said thoughtfully. "But I'll let you know."

"Thanks Martha," Sarah said with a smile. Vicky smiled at her too as she walked up behind Sarah.

"Just wanted to say goodnight," she said to her sister as she paused beside her.

"I can't believe how fast the day has gone by," Sarah shook her head and glanced at her watch. "Guess it is wedding season!"

"It sure is," Vicky sighed with a laugh. Wedding season was solidly booked with guests, weddings, parties and receptions. It was their busiest time of year. "Get home safe, okay?" Vicky gave her sister a quick hug.

"Do you want to come for dinner?" Sarah suggested. Vicky considered the idea of being splattered with spinach by Rory, the two year old with fantastic aim, and then shook her head slightly.

"Not tonight, I need to do a little extra work on the wedding," she mumbled. She loved her nephews dearly but did not relish the idea of sharing the dinner table with them tonight.

***

That night as she settled into her apartment on the first floor of the inn, she considered Sarah and Henry's words regarding firing Bob. She knew that they were both right. Bob wasn't contributing anything positive to the inn, in fact she spent more time cleaning up after the mistakes he made. The decision had to be made, and she would have to fire him. But how?

She lay awake that night, thinking of just how to tell Bob that he would have to find a new job. She didn't like the idea of having to do it, but she knew that it was her responsibility. It was at times like that, when she had so much on her mind, that she did kind of wish she had someone in her life that she could turn to. She was sure Mitchell would understand her conflict, since working as a deputy sheriff was not exactly a glorious career. But he had not called her. That caused her to run through the date for the thousandth time in her mind. She just couldn't place where things might have gone sour. She had thought they enjoyed each other's company. Having said that, she had not called him either. That was one of those relationship games that she couldn't grasp the concept of. Who was supposed to call who?

Vicky sighed and nestled her head deeper into her pillow. She thought of her parents and how their lives had been cut short so suddenly. She didn't want the same to happen to her, before she even had the chance to truly live. Aunt Ida had become very eccentric after Vicky's parents' death, and one late evening when just she and Vicky were still awake sharing memories, she admitted that it was because she wanted to live her life to the fullest. She no longer wanted to let her fears or hesitations limit her. After all, no one ever knew how much time they would have left.

At some point during the night Vicky must have fallen asleep, because she woke up to sunlight pouring in through her window. Her apartment which was in its own section of the inn faced the back gardens, and it was always a beautiful sight to see first thing in the morning. She awoke with the certainty of what she had to do. There was no putting it off any longer. She would have to find a replacement for Bob, but even before she did the gardens would be better off if they had no gardener at all than to have Bob poisoning all of the plants by over watering them or clipping the wrong things. She showered and dressed in a simple business suit, then paused in front of the mirror and looked herself straight in the eye.

"You can do this," she said to herself with forced confidence. "You are a professional, and Bob is not living up to his promise to do a good job. Firing someone does not make you a bad person," Vicky nodded at her own reflection as if she agreed. Then she marched down the hall to the door that led out to the back gardens. First she went to the staff quarters, fully expecting that Bob would still be sleeping. But he did not answer the door. She knocked a few more times before deciding he really wasn't there. Then she began wandering through the gardens on the off chance that he might actually be working. She saw his handiwork all right, from beheaded flowers to trampled grass. She was sure he had no idea how to actually be a gardener, yet another thing that he had lied to her about.

As she walked through one of the largest gardens which featured a beautiful rose garden, she caught her foot on something. As she stumbled she first assumed it might be a root or a stone. But when she looked down it was not a root or a stone. It was a shoe. Her gaze followed the shoe right up a pant leg, and across a plaid shirt, to the face of the man that she had intended to fire that very morning. It looked as if she would not be dealing with that problem after all, but something much worse.

When the blood curdling scream carried through the air, Vicky thought at first that Aunt Ida must have found another spider, until she realized that it was pouring from her own lips. Bob was dead, that much was clear, and it had been no accident, that was very obvious by the splashed blood which was clinging to roses, leaves and flower blossoms. Sarah and Aunt Ida came rushing out of the inn when they heard the scream. When they ran up to her, Vicky was still screaming and didn't even realize it, she was in such shock. Aunt Ida wrapped her arms around her and pulled her close, turning her head away from the gruesome discovery.

"Don't look at it, don't look," Aunt Ida insisted as she rocked her niece slightly in her arms. Sarah whipped out her cell phone with trembling hands and began dialing the police.

"Is that Bob?" she asked anxiously. "How did this happen?"

"Yes," Vicky managed to choke out. "I don't know! I just found him like this!"

"Did you see anyone running away?" Sarah asked, her eyes flicking around the garden in search of anyone that might be responsible for the crime. They could all be in danger if the killer was still around.

"No," Vicky wept as she leaned heavily on her

Aunt's shoulder. "I just found him like this. I came looking for him to fire him, and then I found him like this," her shoulders trembled as another sob ran through her. She had never found someone in that condition before, and it was very disturbing to think that she had a conversation with him just the day before.

"Get inside," Sarah said sternly as she waited for the police to come on the line. "We need to lock the doors and make sure all the guests are secure. Whoever did this might still be on the property!"

Vicky gasped as she had never thought of that. She and Aunt Ida hurried into the inn with Sarah following right behind them. She gave the information to the police over the phone while the three of them went door to door in the inn making sure all of the exterior doors were locked. Within just a few minutes they heard sirens charging up the long, winding driveway that led to the inn. The police station was situated between the inn and downtown, so they did not have far to go. When they saw the flashing lights the sisters felt it was safe enough to step outside.

Sarah and Vicky stood on the front porch of the inn and watched as the officers piled out of their cars and began scouring the property. Some even had their guns drawn. It was a very strange sight to see in such a beautiful setting. The garden where Bob's body was found was quickly roped off with bright yellow police tape. The guests at the inn began asking lots of questions about what was happening as they gathered in the lobby, drawn by the flashing lights of the police cruisers.

Luckily there weren't too many guests at the inn as it was the middle of the week, but they would be packed full by the time the weekend arrived. Timothy, the man who Sarah had checked in the day before, walked right through the lobby area and out onto the porch. He paused beside the two women and narrowed his eyes as he looked over at the police. Vicky braced herself for the questions that he might ask, but he only offered a mild shrug. Then without a word he continued down the steps and to his car.

Deputy Sheriff Mitchell Slate came jogging up to the porch, his eyes wide with concern as he looked from Vicky to Sarah and then back again.

"I'm so sorry for your trouble," he said politely as he removed his hat in a courteous if not archaic display of manners. "Are you two ladies all right?"

"Yes, just shaken up," Sarah replied nervously, her voice more shrill than normal. She still had an arm wrapped around Vicky's shoulders, though Vicky had begun to regain her composure.

"There are a few questions I need to ask you," he explained apologetically. "Who found the body?" Mitchell asked, trying to keep his voice professional yet still compassionate. He was a very handsome man who had been transferred from the deep south. He still called women ma'am and had a way of gazing at people with such deep respect that it was just a shade boyish. Vicky found it to be very endearing, especially when paired with the fierce blue of his eyes. He had strong features with a square jawline and a prominent, sloped nose. His sandy brown hair was mussed by his hat, and splayed across his forehead in many different directions.

"I did," Vicky said hesitantly, she hated to think of it.

"Oh," Mitchell pulled out his notebook and flipped it open. He began to scribble notes down in it. "And how did you happen to find it?" he asked without looking up at her.

"I was looking for Bob, he's our gardener," Vicky explained haltingly, her heart pounding. Mitchell glanced up at her furtively and then back at the notepad he was holding.

"Were the two of you supposed to meet?" he asked, his voice even and solely professional now.

"No," Vicky shook her head slightly. "I had something I needed to tell him," she said hesitantly. She really didn't want to admit that she was about to fire the poor man.

"Were you lovers?" Mitchell asked abruptly, causing Vicky to gasp slightly in disgust.

"No, of course not," she shook her head dismissively. "I was looking for him to fire him."

"I'm sorry," Mitchell said quickly. "It's just one of the first questions we always ask in the case of a homicide," he reached up and perched his hat back on top of his head so he could continue to take notes. "Did you notice anything out of the ordinary this morning?" he asked, still avoiding looking directly at her.

"No," Vicky said firmly, she had been through it many times in her mind. "I just walked into the garden, and I..." her voice broke off slightly. She had never experienced anything so disturbing before.

"It's okay," Mitchell said gently and reached out to softly caress her shoulder.

"Deputy Slate," the sheriff called from behind him in a sharp no nonsense tone. Sheriff McDonnell was a surly looking man. He had a round belly that caused his tan uniform shirt to be strained and a black mustache that hung limply over his mouth. He wore a broad hat similar to a cowboy and his piercing, brown gaze always seemed to be accusing someone of something.

Mitchell drew his hand back quickly and turned to face the sheriff with a slightly guilty expression.

"Can you tear yourself away from your lady friend long enough to give me an update on the corpse in the garden?" he asked in a short tone. He swept a judging glare over the two sisters.

"Oh, yes of course," Mitchell mumbled and looked over the notes he had made. "Well, he was discovered this morning by Ms. Braydon, and so far that is all we really know. It does look like he was bludgeoned with something, maybe a shovel, or a baseball bat."

"How awful," Sarah winced at the details and tugged lightly at Vicky's arm. "Maybe we should go inside, and get out of the officers way so that they can clear out the body."

"Wait just a minute," the sheriff called out as he stomped up the steps of the front porch.

"First of all, no one is moving that body until all of the forensic evidence is collected," he said sternly.

"But Sheriff I have a wedding set to take place in that garden this weekend," Vicky protested, her eyes wide with surprise. She had assumed they would be done with their investigation by the end of the day.

"I'm sorry if this poor fellow's misfortune has caused you any trouble," the sheriff said rather rudely and narrowed his eyes. "Now from what I understand from questioning the other employees, there weren't too many people that actually liked this fellow Bob. Did the two of you have anything you were arguing about?"

Vicky's eyes widened at the idea that the sheriff was actually questioning her, as if she might somehow be involved.

"Of course not. I hired him as a favor, and he simply wasn't good at his job, so I was going to fire him," she frowned as she realized that could very well paint her as a suspect. Then Vicky suddenly remembered the argument that Bob had had with the chef. Was it possible that it had continued after she left? Did they fight so badly that it had ended in murder? She couldn't imagine Henry ever doing something like that. But maybe Bob had confronted his brother, or maybe his brother had finally hunted him down.

"Did you notice anyone suspicious around this morning, or maybe yesterday?" the sheriff asked, taking over the questioning for Deputy Slate who asked a few questions of Sarah about the property itself.

"No," Vicky said carefully, and then she thought better of it. She didn't want to be accused of withholding information. "Well, he did mention he had a falling out with his brother over some money he owed him. Apparently his brother had been trying to find him."

"I see," the sheriff nodded to Mitchell for him to make a note of her words, which Mitchell did.

"We'll make sure that we look into that. Now would you mind showing us where the shovels and other tools might be stored. Maybe our murderer used a shovel and decided to put it back where he got it from," Sheriff McDonnell said hopefully. He wanted the case to be solved before lunch.

"The garden shed is just around back," Vicky began to explain to him. The sheriff smiled at her in a way that was not at all friendly.

"Why don't you show us?" he suggested with thinning patience. The last thing Vicky wanted to do was walk back through that garden. But she knew that the sheriff already had something against her, so she decided to cooperate as much as possible.

"I'll go with you," Sarah suggested quickly when she saw the discomfort in her sister's expression.

"No it's all right, you take care of the guests," Vicky said to Sarah as she walked down the front steps. Mitchell followed closely after her.

"Don't worry Sarah, I'll stay with her," he assured Sarah.

"Yes, and do get me a list of your guests please

40

Sarah," the sheriff requested sternly. "I want to know everyone who checked in or out in the past week, understand?"

Sarah nodded and stepped back into the inn. Vicky walked carefully through the garden with Mitchell remaining closely at her side. She kept an eye out for anything else she might trip over.

"This is the shed," she said as she stopped beside a large wooden structure. "Oh," she murmured as she looked closely at the lock. "Well, that's strange," she started to reach for the lock, but Mitchell grabbed her hand before she could. His touch inspired a quick increase in her heartbeat that startled her. He had noticed that the lock was broken as well.

"Fingerprints," he explained as he quickly released her hand and ducked his head to hide a blush. He nodded to one of the gloved officers who carefully opened the door to the shed. Inside it looked as if a tornado had struck. Everything that was normally neatly stored on the shelves that lined the walls had been tossed down onto the floor. Pots and bags of soil were overturned and even ripped open. Buckets had been emptied out all over the floor. It was such a mess that Vicky wouldn't even know where to begin to clean it up.

"Seems like someone was looking for something," Mitchell said quietly as his gaze stroked over the horrible mess.

"The question is, did he find what he was looking for?" the sheriff wondered out loud as he peeked in the garden shed from behind them. "I think this is going to be one long investigation," he sighed and pulled out his phone. "Better let the wife know."

Mitchell met Vicky's eyes as she stood outside the garden shed. He frowned as he studied her.

"I'm glad you didn't get hurt," he said quietly. "Who knows what could have happened if you walked into the garden in the middle of the attack."

Vicky smiled faintly at his concern. She still had a hard time reading what his intentions were, but it was nice to know that he cared.

"Actually, it looks like this man was killed sometime in the late evening last night," one of the assistants to the Medical Examiner said as he walked up to the sheriff to give him the information.

"Do you have a time of death?" the sheriff

asked as he hung up his phone.

"Approximately midnight," the man said with a slight nod. "Could be an hour either side."

"Thanks," the sheriff said and looked directly at Vicky. "I want to speak to all of your guests, now," he stated flatly. "Someone may have seen or heard something."

"Oh Sheriff, do you think that's really necessary?" Vicky pleaded.

"Oh no, it's fine," the sheriff shrugged mildly, his tone biting. "We'll just let the murderer walk free so that your high end customers don't get ruffled," he glowered at her.

"Excuse me?" Vicky began to say, offended by his tone, but Mitchell stepped boldly between them.

"I'll take care of the questioning Sheriff," he said respectfully. "I'm sure we can find a non-intrusive way to handle this," he assured Vicky as he glanced over his shoulder at her. Vicky was a little startled by how close he was standing to her, but she nodded at his words. She knew that he would be a lot more polite when talking to the guests.

"Fine," she agreed as she took one last look at

the messy garden shed.

"But first we need to search Bob's room, and I want to speak to any staff that might have had an issue with him," the sheriff insisted.

Vicky bit into her bottom lip as she realized that was going to include Henry. She knew she had no choice but to tell the truth, so she pulled Mitchell gently aside.

"Listen, Bob didn't work here for very long, but he did have a few run ins with the chef, Henry. Just little things, like him being unhappy about the vegetables rotting in the garden because Bob didn't harvest them, and Bob's brother apparently confronted Henry when he was looking for Bob. But Henry is a good man, and I know he wouldn't do this," she met his gaze, hoping that he would believe her.

Mitchell studied her and then he wrote down the details of her statement. He tucked his notebook into his back pocket and smiled warmly at her.

"Don't worry Vicky, all of this will be over soon. I'll make sure I get the whole story from Henry. It looks like Bob's brother will be the prime suspect. Maybe that's what he was looking for in the garden shed, the money that his brother owed him. Did Bob ever mention how much he owed?"

"No," Vicky sighed quietly as she studied the scene unfolding before her. She felt regretful for not prying more into Bob's business. Maybe if she had, she would have found a way to prevent all of this.

***

While Mitchell was questioning the guests inside the inn, and the sheriff was searching Bob's room in the employees' quarters, Aunt Ida stepped outside to join Vicky.

"Look at all these handsome police officers," Aunt Ida whispered in Vicky's ear. "I love a man in uniform!"

Vicky frowned as she leaned closer to Aunt Ida and whispered back. "Bob was definitely murdered in the garden!"

"Are you serious?" Aunt Ida gasped with horror and just a little bit of delight. "Well, isn't that just grand!" she declared, her eyes shimmering.

"What?" Vicky asked with shock in her voice as she turned to look at her aunt. She wanted to be sure that she had heard her correctly. Grand was not how she would describe the situation.

"Well, I mean it's not grand for Bob of course," Ida frowned as if she was offering the correct amount of grief for the man she barely knew. "He did rescue me from a spider," she said with a nod of respect. "But just think, our very own murder mystery."

"Aunt Ida this is not one of your books," Vicky pointed out with a shake of her head. Aunt Ida had an affection for all things mysterious. She was always reading murder mysteries, though half the time she fell asleep after a few pages. She always said she didn't care, because she had the crime solved in the first few paragraphs.

"No it's better," Aunt Ida insisted with a grim smile as she looked over the gathering of police officers. "Besides if we don't solve the murder, who will? You know none of these boys have any idea what to do about a homicide."

Vicky considered that as she studied the mostly young men who were idly chatting with one another. Aunt Ida had a point. She couldn't remember the last time there was an actual homicide in their small town. This made it even more unlikely that she would be able to have the wedding on the weekend. She was going to have a very disappointed bride on her hands.

"You may be right," Vicky said quietly. "Maybe if we just help out a little by looking into things, we can get this case solved in time for the Merriam wedding."

"Oh yes, I'm sure we can," Aunt Ida nodded, pleased that Vicky was agreeing to her plan. "With you and I on the case how could we ever go wrong?"

Vicky laughed and shook her head as she slid her arm through her aunt's. "I don't think we could."

"So where do we start?" Aunt Ida wondered. "Should we question the witnesses, search for evidence, or consult a psychic?"

"Well, the garden shed was ransacked, as if someone was looking for something," Vicky said thoughtfully. "I'm willing to bet that they didn't find what they were looking for."

"Hmm, maybe we should have a second look?" Aunt Ida suggested with a gleam in her eyes.

"Maybe there's something they missed?"

"It's such a mess I don't think we could find anything," Vicky shook her head slightly. "Actually with everyone being questioned by the police, I think it might be a good idea if I did a check of all the rooms and make sure that nothing else has been destroyed or is missing."

"You do that," Aunt Ida agreed with a smile as she began to walk towards the garden shed. "I'll just take a second look!"

Vicky shook her head in amazement at her aunt. Most people would want to run away from a crime scene, but she couldn't wait to dive in. When Vicky stepped into the inn she saw Sarah looking very frazzled as she tried to explain to each guest what was happening and that they were not in any danger. From the look in her eyes Vicky could surmise that many were asking for refunds or discounts on their stay because of the disruption.

Vicky knew it was terrible for business to have the police presence but she was secretly glad that they were there. It still lurked in the back of her mind that there was a slim possibility that the murderer really could be one of the guests at the inn. She didn't believe it could be one of the employees, but a lot of people did come and go at the inn. Even if it wasn't a guest, there were plenty of places for a murderer to hide out in such a vast building. At least she hoped that with all the police presence the culprit would have been scared off. As Vicky walked the halls on the second and third floors she didn't see anything out of the ordinary. She checked all the empty rooms to be sure that no one was hiding out inside.

Then she decided to head for the staff quarters, where she knew the sheriff should be done searching Bob's room. A few other staff members also shared the building, including the chef Henry, and three of the maids who chose to take advantage of the discounted rent and be very close to work. As she expected, the sheriff was finished with the search in Bob's room, but as Vicky walked down the hallway towards the maids' quarters, she was surprised to find that Henry's door was ajar. It was not just open, but it looked as if it had been forced open.

How had the police overlooked this? Vicky had not seen Henry all morning, so when she pushed gently on the door she wasn't sure what she would find. She hoped that it wouldn't be anything as devastating as what she had found in the garden. What she found was that Henry's room had been ransacked. Everything was torn from the walls and there was broken glass on the floor. Vicky knew she should call for one of the officers who would still be nearby, but she was drawn into the scene, her heart pounding. She just kept hoping that Henry was safe.

Vicky stepped further in, more carefully, as she knew that the sheriff would want to be notified about a new crime scene and that she could be treading on evidence. As she did, she felt a little uneasy. Something seemed off, beyond the mess, and she just couldn't place what it was. She drew a shaky breath and noticed that the mattress on the bed was pushed aside. Someone had even run a knife through the mattress. The sight of the torn mattress made her even more nervous. Whoever had done this was certainly armed.

Again Vicky felt as if she should be noticing something. Then it struck her, the room was silent. But she could hear something. It sounded distinctly like breathing. Then she heard the squeak of the closet door swinging open. Before she could spin all the way around to face whoever was leaping out of the closet, something hard and heavy struck her on the back of the head. She slumped forward into the broken glass and other rubble on the floor, the pain searing through her before she completely blacked out. One image burned into her mind as she slipped into darkness.

Chapter Three

"Have you seen Vicky?" Aunt Ida asked as she walked through the kitchen. Henry shook his head, his cheeks flush with annoyance. He was angrily chopping vegetables with a large knife.

"No, but I certainly talked to enough police officers this morning. As if I would ever murder someone," he shook his head with disgust. Aunt Ida fixed him with a steady gaze.

"Well, where were you last night Henry?" she asked as any good detective would.

"I was here!" Henry scoffed. "I had to go to the market and buy fresh vegetables since that buffoon," he paused a moment and sighed. "Forgive me for speaking ill of the dead, but he murdered all the vegetables in the garden! So I had to work late to get breakfast prepared for this morning."

"Oh I see," Aunt Ida nodded and glanced around the kitchen. His alibi would be easy enough to prove as there was a surveillance camera leading in and out of the kitchen. As long as he was seen walking into the kitchen before midnight and not walking out before midnight, then he was in the clear. She of course wouldn't be convinced until she saw the video for herself. But that wasn't what she was concerned about at the moment.

"Can you believe all of this?" Sarah asked as she walked into the kitchen from the other direction. "We're going to lose a lot of business over this," she sighed and shook her head as the numbers swam through her mind. "And then I have to wonder, are we really safe here?" she asked in a more fearful voice.

"Bob brought this here," Henry said sharply as he laid the knife down on the cutting board. "He owed people money and was associating with the wrong sort of people. We've never had any trouble here, before he came," he scowled.

"Now Henry," Aunt Ida said in a chastising tone. "The poor man is dead, I don't think being angry at him is going to make it any worse for him."

Henry sighed and nodded as he swept the vegetables into a large metal bowl.

"Sarah, have you seen Vicky?" Aunt Ida asked as she stepped closer to her niece.

"I thought she was with you?" Sarah asked

with surprise.

"Oh I'm sure she's just off investigating," Ida shrugged as if it was nothing to be worried about, but she was worried. She hadn't been able to find Vicky for some time, and they had planned to meet back up.

"I wonder where she could be," Sarah said as she walked towards the large kitchen window. "It's not like her to just disappear, especially with all of this going on."

"I checked her apartment, but she wasn't there," Aunt Ida explained, her voice beginning to show her concern. "I'm afraid she might have taken my advice to investigate this crime ourselves a little too seriously."

"I'd say so," Sarah frowned with exasperation. "Aunt Ida, you two should not be meddling in this. A horrible crime has been committed here, and we don't even have any idea who might have done it. The murderer could still be somewhere close by. This is a job for the police to do, not for the two of you to get in the middle of." Sometimes she felt as if she was mothering her Aunt.

Ida hung her head. "I know," she murmured

and then glanced up at Sarah. "But with the wedding coming up, we just thought it would be best to figure all this out as fast as we could."

Sarah was still staring out the window, which overlooked the staff quarters, when she saw Vicky stumbling out of one of the rooms.

"There she is!" Sarah called out, and then gasped in horror when she saw a trickle of blood trailing down her sister's forehead. "Oh no she's hurt!"

Aunt Ida and Sarah ran out of the kitchen. Sarah called back over her shoulder for Henry to call for some of the remaining police officers. Most had left as they had collected all the evidence they could, but Mitchell had insisted that a few officers remain to put the guests and staff at ease. As the two women ran to Vicky she was leaning against the front wall of the building to keep herself steady. Her vision was swimming and she was having a hard time standing upright. She had a few flecks of glass stuck to her cheek from collapsing on the floor. Her head hurt terribly, and she recalled being struck on the back of the head, but mostly she was confused. Had she really seen what she thought she saw?

"I need to see the sheriff," she said, her voice slightly slurred as she was still recovering from the blow. Two officers came running up to them, their hands on their holstered weapons.

"Are you okay?" one asked as he looked at the blood on Vicky's forehead. It was just from a small cut, likely from glass.

"Someone attacked me," Vicky breathed out, every word making her head hurt more. "He was hiding, and he attacked me, but he's gone now," she pointed in the direction of Henry's room. The officers went quickly to search it.

"Let's get you inside," Aunt Ida said nervously as she glanced around. It was still possible that the culprit was lingering nearby.

"What happened?" Sarah demanded as she eased her sister into the kitchen and sat her down at the table.

"The killer," Vicky explained breathlessly. "He was here, he was in Henry's room!"

"What?" Henry asked as he hurried over to Vicky with a wet rag to staunch the bleeding from the cut on her forehead. He knocked the knife off of the counter. It clattered into the metal sink, making them all jump with surprise at the sharp sound. "Are you sure?" he asked.

"Yes, he was hiding in your closet," Vicky said and winced at how much it hurt to talk. "I need to talk to the sheriff, I saw something important."

"He's on his way," Sarah assured her. Once the cut had been cleaned, Henry headed for the freezer and gathered some ice. He walked over with a bag of ice wrapped in a towel for the knot on the back of her head. Aunt Ida was looking at the wound on the back of Vicky's head closely.

"She's got quite a bump," Aunt Ida declared with anger in her voice. "But it looks like she will be okay."

"We'll let the paramedics decide that," Sarah said firmly, she wasn't taking any chances.

"Paramedics, no," Vicky shook her head groggily. "Really I'm fine."

"You certainly are not fine," Mitchell corrected from the door of the kitchen. He walked towards Vicky with a deep frown. "What happened?" he asked in a whisper when he noticed the small cut on her forehead.

"It's just from glass," Vicky said swiftly. "Henry's room was broken into. So I went in to have a look..."

"Why?" Mitchell demanded, his eyes full of concern. "Why would you walk in instead of calling me?"

Vicky lowered her eyes as she realized now how stupid she was to go in.

"I just figured I might be able to find something," she said quietly. "I was worried that Henry was hurt."

"Then what happened?" Mitchell asked her in a more gentle tone as he noted the fear that rose in her eyes.

"Yes, fill us in," the sheriff requested as he walked in behind Mitchell. "Please do tell us all why you felt the need to contaminate a crime scene instead of allowing the good officers of the law do their job?" his eyes were flashing as he glared at Vicky. "You're lucky you're able to talk to us at all young lady."

Vicky frowned at his strong tone. She wasn't a big fan of the sheriff as he always seemed to be angry about something, but in this case she couldn't really argue with him. She had been quite reckless.

"He was hiding in Henry's closet," she said

softly, trying to prevent her head from throbbing with each word she spoke. The paramedics had arrived right behind the police and they were evaluating the bump on the back of Vicky's head.

"So you saw his face?" the sheriff asked hopefully.

"No," Vicky sighed with disappointment as she knew that would have been the most helpful. "I tried to look at him, but he hit me before I could see his face."

"Then how do you know it's a he?" the sheriff demanded. "You must have seen something," he insisted. "Think about it."

"I did," Vicky said firmly as she tried to gather her thoughts. "It struck me as very strange. I saw his arm, which was definitely a man's arm, and he had the same tattoo as Bob!"

"A tattoo?" the sheriff shook his head slightly. "You're probably just confused Vicky. You might have mixed two memories together. Bob is dead, and I highly doubt whoever killed him would just happen to have the exact same tattoo. I think you need some rest."

With that he turned and strode out of the kitchen. "I'm going to search the contaminated crime scene," he called back over his shoulder.

One of the paramedics patted Vicky's hand gently. "This looks like it will be fine with some ice," she said with a compassionate smile. "But we can always take you in to check for a concussion."

"No thank you," Vicky said firmly. "I'm feeling much better, I think I just need some water and a chance to clear my head."

Aunt Ida hurried to get her a glass of water, while Sarah and Henry spoke quietly about what the killer might have been looking for in his room.

Once Mitchell was sure that the sheriff was gone, he turned back to Vicky. He lowered his voice and leaned in close to her.

"Listen, I'm not supposed to tell you this, but I think you need to know, because I want you to realize what you're up against here," he said, his voice heavy with concern.

"What is it?" Vicky asked curiously as the pain began to subside beneath the ice she was holding against her head.

"We checked into Bob thoroughly and it looks like he was recently in jail for burglary," he frowned as he added, "with a deadly weapon."

Vicky's eyes widened at that revelation. "I had no idea," she said as she shook her head. "He said he had fallen on some hard times, and he just needed an income. I didn't realize that those hard times, were actually him doing hard time."

"Yes, it was a longer sentence but it got reduced. He had just got out of jail before he came here. Also we've questioned his brother, but he has an alibi for last night, so we don't think it could be him. We're back to square one on suspects, which means anyone could be the killer," he sighed as he looked deeply into Vicky's eyes. "Look, I know that maybe you didn't enjoy our date too much..."

"What?" Vicky asked with surprise at his words. "Why would you say that?"

"Well," he hesitated and glanced around to be sure that no one else was listening in on their conversation as it did not qualify as official police business, and the sheriff would not be pleased that the discussion was taking place. "You never called, so I just assumed," he explained quietly. "I know I'm not the most exciting person in the world."

"Mitchell," Vicky groaned as she started to shake her head and then stopped because of the bolt of pain the movement ignited. "I was waiting for you to call me," she said with a lopsided grin. She felt very silly for all the times she had checked her phone now. She wondered if Mitchell had been checking his phone just as often.

"Really?" Mitchell's eyes lit up for a moment, then he cleared his throat as he remembered exactly what he was there for. "Well, what I was trying to say was, I'm telling you all this, because, Bob was a very dangerous individual who was involved with other very dangerous individuals. I don't want to see you get hurt, more than you already have, understand?" he arched an eyebrow slightly. Vicky couldn't help but smile at how sweet he was. He was concerned about her, but he was still not being open about it, he was just giving her all of the facts.

"I understand," Vicky said softly. "But, you should understand that I have a very anxious bride who is going to be calling me every single hour on the hour until that crime scene tape comes down, because her wedding is scheduled for this weekend. So, even though I get that I am not a police officer, if there's some way I can help the investigation, I am more than happy to contribute."

Mitchell sat back in his chair and sighed as he studied her. He admired Vicky's strong personality and her determination, but he wondered if that would get her into some serious trouble.

"Just promise me, that if you come across something, and you're not sure if it's dangerous or not, or if it might be important to the investigation, that you call me first, okay?" he suggested.

"I will," Vicky assured him and reached out to lightly touch the back of his hand. "I'm sorry that we had a misunderstanding after our date. I really would like to see you again sometime."

Mitchell smiled as he closed his hand over hers and gave it a gentle squeeze. "I'd like that too," he nodded.

"All right, Bob's room was ransacked as well so we've got the forensics team going through both rooms right now," the sheriff announced as he walked back into the kitchen with an officer behind him. The officer walked Henry out of the kitchen to obtain a list of valuables that might be missing from his room. Vicky swiftly drew her hand away from Mitchell, knowing that if the sheriff spotted the gesture, he might be upset with his deputy sheriff. "It's going to take some time for the results to come back. Until then, stay out of the staff quarters, and if you see anything suspicious, do me a favor and call the people with badges and guns, hmm?" he eyed Vicky with a paternal glare. Vicky forced a smile to her lips and nodded slightly.

"I think I've learned my lesson," she lied, knowing that she was more determined than ever to find out who had attacked her and killed Bob. After all how could she be expected to feel safe until whoever had hurt her was behind bars? When Henry returned to the kitchen, looking stunned by how his room had been destroyed, she was reminded of just how real this situation was.

"Henry, you can stay in the inn," Vicky suggested in a kind tone.

"Sure there are plenty of empty rooms now," Sarah sighed, her shoulders slumping. Several of the guests had opted to leave early due to the investigation, and she couldn't blame them. After all, the entire time they had all assumed that the killer was long gone, he had been lurking in Henry's closet. Was he still hiding somewhere?

"How do we know he's not still on the property?" Sarah asked with a slight shudder.

"I have my officers doing a thorough search," the sheriff said with confidence. "If they don't find him on the premises, then he isn't here. However, you should all be cautious, because he could very well come back. This place is large and it's going to be impossible to keep it secure."

Vicky and Sarah nodded at his words. With so many sprawling gardens, small outbuildings, and many rooms, the inn was a perfect hiding place. Aunt Ida walked over to the kitchen window and stared out wistfully at the staff's quarters.

"Just have to wonder what he could have been looking for," she said to herself, her mind racing as she tried to unravel the mystery. "What could be so important that it would warrant taking the life of another person?"

"Are you sure you don't want to come and stay with Phil and me tonight?" Sarah asked Vicky and Aunt Ida with a frown. "I hate to think of you being all alone here. I think it would be better if we were all together."

'We won't be alone," Vicky said firmly as she pushed herself up from the table. "Aunt Ida will stay with me tonight, won't you?" she asked, and glanced over at Aunt Ida.

"Of course," Aunt Ida agreed. "Didn't I ever tell you girls that I have a black belt in Jujitsu?" she smiled proudly. Both sisters stared at her with wide eyes at those words. It wasn't too much of a stretch for Vicky to imagine Aunt Ida flipping someone right over her shoulder, despite her diminutive size. She wouldn't put anything past Aunt Ida.

***

Aunt Ida settled into Vicky's apartment that night, but she didn't seem very comfortable. Vicky could tell that she was not at all pleased with how plain it was. She could see the woman's mind spinning with ways she could brighten it up and make it more fun to live in. But she was tactful enough to keep it to herself.

"Are you okay sweetie?" she asked Vicky as she glanced in her niece's direction. "Do you want some water or an aspirin for your head?"

"No, it's not too bad really," Vicky said with a small smile. It did hurt, but it did not hurt as bad as it had earlier. She was feeling a lot clearer in her mind as well.

"We can't let this chump get away with this kind of behavior," Aunt Ida said fiercely as she began to pace back and forth across the carpet. "We have to figure out who it is!"

"I know," Vicky said as she watched her aunt pace. "But we have no idea who he is. All I know for sure is that he had the same tattoo that I saw on Bob's arm, that awful one with the snake and the blade," she scrunched up her nose at the memory of it.

"Well, maybe they're friends," Aunt Ida suggested and then laughed at her own words. "Well I guess not anymore."

"Aunt Ida," Vicky sighed and tried not to encourage her aunt. She tended to say some rather inappropriate things.

"We're alone now so we don't have to pretend that we're all upset. Bob wasn't exactly a good person," she reminded Vicky as she sat down beside her on the plain brown couch.

"Maybe not," Vicky said quietly. "But he was still a person, and he didn't deserve to be killed."

"Then the best thing we can do is figure out what happened, and get this guy in jail," Aunt Ida said firmly as she clenched her hands into fists. "We just need a place to start. What about that strange fellow, the one who checked in recently?" Aunt Ida suggested.

"You mean Timothy?" Vicky shook her head slightly as she had suspected the man as well. She had even asked Mitchell about him.

"Mitchell said Timothy told him he was in the lounge all night, and the bartender who worked last night said he was serving Timothy until almost two in the morning," she sighed as yet another suspect was crossed off the list. "So he may be a drinker, but not a killer."

Aunt Ida looked just as disappointed to hear the news. "Well, there has to be something that can give us a clue as to who the killer might be," Aunt Ida said thoughtfully.

"Maybe we can take a look around the garden tomorrow and see if there are any clues that the police missed," Vicky said with a mild shrug. "But Mitchell was right, we need to be very careful. Whoever this person is he could have killed me today if he wanted to, and I don't think he'll be giving out any second chances."

"Absolutely," Aunt Ida nodded. "We'll make sure we are very cautious. Speaking of Mitchell," she added without even taking a breath between her words. "Isn't he just the handsomest young man that you've ever seen?" she asked with a twinkle in her eye. "And he sure does seem to like you."

"Don't get any ideas Aunt Ida," Vicky warned as she met her gaze. "We only went on one date. He's a very nice man, but I'm not looking for anything too serious," Vicky reminded her firmly.

"Oh sweetie," Aunt Ida chuckled, as if Vicky was a well meaning child. "No one looks for serious, serious finds them," she winked lightly at her and then yawned. She stretched out her arms above her head. "I think I'm going to turn in for the night. Are you sure it's all right for me to use your bed?"

"Yes it is," Vicky said firmly. She couldn't even imagine putting her aunt on the couch. "I'll feel better knowing that I'm closer to the door in case anyone tries to get in," Vicky added, her voice breaking slightly with the fear that was randomly bubbling up within her.

"Good night," Aunt Ida kissed her gently on the forehead. Vicky smiled a little at the affectionate caress. It meant so much to her to still have that from someone. Without Aunt Ida she was sure that she and Sarah would not have been able to recover from their parents' deaths so easily. As she watched her aunt head off into the bedroom she was reminded of what an amazing woman she was. There was no doubt in her mind that she really did have a black belt, and that she wasn't afraid to use it. Though Aunt Ida had never married or had children of her own, her life seemed to be very full with stories of places and people that she would never forget.

As Vicky curled up on the couch she tried to think of those memories that Aunt Ida had shared with her instead of the terror she had felt today when she heard that closet door swing open. She hadn't admitted it to anyone, but she was scared that the man would come back. Would he decide that he needed to finish the job? Her fear was all the more reason to continue to pursue the investigation with her aunt. If she had to wait on the police to capture the suspect she might not live to see it.

As she drifted off to sleep her mind was filled with a mixture of all of Aunt Ida's adventures and that shadowy figure striking her from behind. Her dream was all about a snake that was chasing after a man carrying a blade. The snake never seemed to be able to catch up, and the blade glimmered in the sun. Vicky was terrified in the dream. She was certain that the snake was about to turn around and attack her. But no matter how afraid she was, she kept chasing after the snake!

***

She woke the next morning with a start. Her heart was pounding. She thought that she had heard that closet squeak again. She sat up on the couch and looked at the front door. It was still closed and locked.

"Aunt Ida?" she called out. Aunt Ida poked her head out of the kitchen and smiled.

"Just getting some coffee on," she called out cheerfully. Vicky sighed in relief as she was sure that the sound she had heard was the cabinets in the kitchen, not someone breaking into her apartment. She hurried to get dressed for the day, eager to see what they might be able to discover in the garden. As they shared their coffee over Vicky's small kitchen table she was reminded of the delicious brew that Henry made for the guests at the inn.

"You know, I probably should talk to Henry," she said thoughtfully. "He may think that we suspect him, like the police did. I just want to make sure that he understands he has our support. I mean this has been frightening for him too, his entire room was turned upside down."

"That's true," Aunt Ida agreed. "I'll start looking in the garden, and you go off and talk to Henry, then meet me there," she smiled in anticipation of the search.

"Are you sure you'll be okay alone?" Vicky said hesitantly.

"Remember," Aunt Ida started to say.

"Right, black belt," Vicky laughed and shook her head. She was relieved that she didn't feel any pain when she did. As she stood up from the table she leaned over to give her aunt a light kiss on the forehead. "Just remember, if you see anything strange, or notice anyone suspicious, come find me or call Mitchell!"

Then she headed out to find Henry. He was staying on the second floor in one of the empty guest rooms. When she knocked on his door, he answered it right away.

"Hi Henry," she said with a small smile. "I just wanted to check on you."

"Thanks," Henry said with a sigh.

"I'm sorry that the police questioned you so much," Vicky explained quickly. "I just wanted you to know that I told Mitchell there was no way you would have been involved."

"I appreciate that," Henry said with a sigh of relief. "It's all right now, I just had a call from one of the officers to let me know that the surveillance cameras proved my alibi. At least I won't be a suspect anymore."

"Oh that's good," Vicky said with a wider smile. "Please, if you need anything, just let me know, okay?"

"Thanks Vicky," he said with genuine gratitude. "I think I'm just going to get a little more rest."

"Okay," she waved lightly to him as he stepped back inside the room and closed the door. As she walked down the hallway on the second floor, a conversation drew her attention. One of the guest room doors was slightly ajar and she paused beside it, listening to the voice inside.

"I couldn't find it," the voice was saying. She recognized it as belonging to Timothy, the man who had checked in just the day before the murder happened. He had a very distinctive quality to his voice, almost an accent but she couldn't quite place it. He had been ruled out as a suspect because he was seen at the inn lounge until well past one in the morning, but now it sounded like he was admitting to being the person who had ransacked the shed, and Bob and Henry's rooms. "I looked everywhere. I even looked in another room in case I had the wrong one, but it wasn't there. Now the police are all over it." It sounded like there was someone else in the room with him, but the voice was too distant for her to hear clearly. It was just a mumble, she couldn't make out any of the words.

Vicky was leaning closer when she saw the knob on the door start to move and knew that soon Timothy would be in the hallway. If he caught her listening in then he might decide to do her harm again, if he was indeed the killer that meant he was also the same person who had attacked her. She ducked into the empty guest room beside his, and waited until she heard the door next door click shut. He hadn't been walking out, but must have just discovered that the door was still open. Her heart was racing as she wondered how this could be possible.

How had it been Timothy who searched the rooms if he had an alibi for the night of the murder? Who had he been talking to in the room? Was it possible that there was more than one killer staying at the inn? She waited until she was certain it was safe and then hurried down to the garden to meet Aunt Ida.

***

Aunt Ida was closely inspecting the soil in the garden, just in case the police had overlooked footprints or any discarded evidence. When she heard Vicky running towards her she looked up swiftly, ready to defend herself against a killer.

Her face fell with relief when she saw that it was Vicky.

"Are you okay?" Aunt Ida called out with concern when she saw Vicky's fast approach and her wide fear filled eyes.

"I think so," Vicky said breathlessly as she came to a stop beside her aunt. "But I just overheard something very strange."

"What was it?" Ida asked, obviously intrigued.

"It was that new guest Timothy. He said that he had searched both rooms but he couldn't find it. It sounded like he was talking to someone else in the room," her mind was spinning as she tried to recover from how fast she was running.

"That is strange," Aunt Ida agreed quietly, her brain was working overtime trying to piece together the clues. "Maybe this whole time we have been thinking too small. Maybe the killer has an accomplice."

"You mean you think there are two criminals on the property?" Vicky nodded and then glanced over her shoulder at the inn behind her. "That's what I was thinking too. We've got to stop this before it gets any worse. If they haven't found what they're looking for, then they're not going to be going anywhere."

"That's why we have to find it first," Aunt Ida pointed out with a slight smile, as if she had found the perfect solution.

"If they couldn't find it, how could we?" Vicky asked with surprise and a bit of trepidation. She didn't like being so close to the man who had attacked her.

"Because they don't know everything there is to know about this place," Aunt Ida pointed out with a smug smile. "Even the police wouldn't have known everything. I bet if the two of us go search Bob's room we'll find something that both the killer and the police overlooked. Let's give it a shot!"

"All right," Vicky agreed, it was true that she had just about every square inch of the place memorized, including the staff's quarters. She would often spend time there with some of the staff, playing cards, or playing with their children. Still walking right back into danger made her a little uneasy. She held up the yellow tape for Aunt Ida. Aunt Ida stepped under, as deftly as a spy, and then ducked into Bob's room. Vicky followed quickly after, and wondered if she was making another mistake.

Vicky decided to call Mitchell as he had asked, and give him this new information that she had overheard. But when she dialed his number, it only rang several times and then went to voicemail. She didn't want to leave a message just in case she turned out to be wrong, after all Timothy could have been talking about something else entirely. Coincidences did happen. As she stepped into Bob's room after Aunt Ida, Vicky hoped that they would find something that could help them solve the case.

"What a mess," Ida was complaining. "How are we ever supposed to find anything in this?" she asked with a frown.

"Well, we need to think smart," Vicky said as she looked over the room. "Both the killer and the police searched through this room and come up empty handed. So it's not going to be hidden in an obvious spot."

"Think about it Vicky," Aunt Ida encouraged her. "Is there anything about this room that you know, that neither the killer nor the police would have the advantage of knowing?"

'Well," Vicky thought about it for a moment.

"Not really. I gave Bob this room to stay in for free because he promised to fix the carpet in the corner that had been torn up when we moved some heavy furniture."

Aunt Ida grinned and snapped her fingers. "That's it!" she said quickly. "Where's the torn up corner?"

Vicky walked over to it, and tugged up the corner. "Bob said he would fix it, but he never did," Vicky said quietly. "I figured it was because he was just too lazy to do it, but maybe it was for another reason," she folded the carpet back, and tucked beneath the edge of it was a small golden key. She plucked it up off the floorboards and held it up for Aunt Ida to see.

"Here it is!" she said with amazement.

"But what is it for?" Aunt Ida asked feeling very confused. "It's just a key. Why would there be all the fuss over a key?"

Before Vicky could answer they heard footsteps on the walkway outside leading up to the door of Bob's room. Vicky's eyes widened, and Aunt Ida held her breath. In mere seconds the killer would discover them in the room. Vicky quickly tucked the key into her bra for safe keeping. Then she grabbed Aunt Ida's hand and led her through the small kitchen in the room, to the back door. As quietly as she could she eased the door open. They slipped out the back door, just in time to hear the front door swing forcibly open.

"He's not going to find it now," Vicky whispered as she and Ida hurried away from the building. "But that's only going to make him angrier. We have to figure out what this key is for before anyone else gets hurt."

Chapter Four

They made their way back into the inn and into Vicky's apartment. Once the door was closed and locked they both looked at each other with fear filled eyes.

"That was close," Aunt Ida breathed.

"Too close," Vicky pointed out, her heart racing so fast that she thought she might pass out. "I've got to sit down," she said as she sank down onto the couch. Her head was still swimming, probably because of the large knot that had formed.

"Do you think it was Timothy?" Aunt Ida asked as she settled down next to Vicky.

"It has to be," Vicky frowned as she tried to get her dizziness to subside. "He almost caught us. If he saw us, then he'll know we're on to him."

"We can't let him know," Aunt Ida insisted. "Do you still have the key? It didn't fall out did it?"

"No it didn't fall out," Vicky replied as she fished the key out of her bra. She held it up in the light so they could take a closer look at it. It was an odd size for a key. It didn't look large enough to open a door.

"I'm going to call Mitchell," Vicky said firmly. "This has got a little out of hand, and I promised him I would call."

"All right," Aunt Ida nodded though she looked a little disappointed. She seemed to really be enjoying the adventure she was having. But then she wasn't the one who had been hit over the head and knocked out. When Vicky dialed Mitchell's phone number, once again it rang and rang and then went to voice mail. Vicky frowned as she checked the number to make sure that it was correct.

"What could he be doing?" she wondered. Just for an instant she considered that maybe he had only told her to call him out of courtesy. Maybe he didn't really want to have to speak to her.

***

"Please sir, this is the second time she's called," Mitchell begged as he looked across the desk at his boss. The sheriff only shook his head and leveled his damning gaze on Mitchell.

"No we don't have time for you to make goo goo eyes with Ms. Braydon," he said gruffly. "We need to figure out who this killer is. I won't have him running loose through my city."

"Well, we've ruled out the chef Henry, and Bob's brother Larry, he was out of town at the time of the crime," he frowned as he looked back down at his phone. He hated ignoring Vicky's calls, but the sheriff had noticed their little hand holding session earlier in the day and had put his foot down about personal calls. "Really sir, I told Vicky to call me if she ran into any trouble, please can I just check in with her?" he pleaded.

"What kind of trouble do you think she ran into?" the sheriff asked with a smile. "Another ghost tattoo?"

"I'm sure she wasn't lying about that," Mitchell argued. He was really starting to lose his temper with the way the sheriff was talking about Vicky. He didn't like it when he disrespected her.

"I didn't say she was lying son," the sheriff corrected him in a fatherly tone. "I said she was mistaken. Nobody takes a whack like that on the noggin and gets up thinking straight. What are the chances that the killer has the same tattoo as

Bob? What were they both part of the same secret club or something?" he chuckled as he shook his head.

Mitchell sighed as he looked back down at his phone. He could only hope that Vicky wasn't in any real trouble.

***

"I guess we're on our own," Vicky shrugged, feeling perplexed. She couldn't understand why Mitchell would tell her to call if he didn't intend to answer the phone.

"That's all right," Aunt Ida insisted with a purr in her tone. "We can handle this all by ourselves. All we need to do is figure out what this key opens."

Vicky studied it intently. She could tell by its size and shape that it opened a small lock.

"I know!" Vicky suddenly said as she jumped up from the couch. "Maybe it goes to one of the safety deposit boxes that we keep in the inn's safe. We offer it to our guests as a way to store their valuables. I didn't think that Bob had one, but this looks to be about the right size."

"Well, let's go check it out!" Aunt Ida insisted. They headed for the back office behind the front desk of the lobby where the safe was kept. Sarah had chosen to stay home for the day since they had very few guests remaining. Vicky knew it was likely because Phil had insisted he didn't want her anywhere near a murderer who might still be at large. They checked carefully for any sign of Timothy before they stepped out into the lobby.

"Look, there he goes!" Vicky pointed out the front window of the lobby. Timothy was striding quickly towards his car. Vicky couldn't help but wonder where he was going, but she was glad that he was leaving.

"Good riddance, maybe he won't come back," Aunt Ida said with a huff. "Even if he is handsome, that doesn't excuse him from being a maniac," she said sternly.

"I wouldn't think so," Vicky said trying to hide a smile at her Aunt's dramatic statement. They hurried into the office and closed the door behind them. Vicky knew the code to the safe so she unlocked it. When she opened the door of the safe she found the safety deposit boxes right where she expected them to be. It didn't look as if they had been disturbed in any way. She tried to slide the key into the lock on the first one, but it wouldn't go in.

"It doesn't fit," she said with a sigh of disappointment. "It must not open these."

"What else could it open?" Aunt Ida asked as she took the key and looked it over closely. There were no numbers or initials on it to indicate what it might open. Vicky carefully locked the safe back up, and then turned to look at the key as well.

"It could be for a storage locker somewhere," Vicky pointed out with a frown. "But it doesn't really look like a locker key."

"Oh I know, maybe it goes to a treasure chest," Aunt Ida suggested with a gleam in her eye.

"You mean like a real treasure chest?" Vicky asked with a slight chuckle. "What would Bob be doing with a key to a treasure chest?" then suddenly she remembered what Mitchell had said about Bob just being released from jail for armed robbery. If the money was never recovered he might have hidden it somewhere. That would explain why such dangerous people were after it. "Oh maybe he had the money stashed somewhere for when he got out!" Vicky said with amazement as the pieces began to fit together. "If he did then he might have tried to hide it in a treasure chest, he might have even buried it!"

Aunt Ida smiled triumphantly. She loved the fact that Vicky could follow along with her ideas.

"So if it is a treasure chest, and it is buried, where is it buried?" Aunt Ida wondered with a frown. "If he went to this much trouble to hide it, then he probably did a good job of burying it. But this property is so huge, we may never be able to find it," she sighed with disappointment. It was not like Aunt Ida to give up on anything, but this task seemed particularly impossible.

Vicky was lost in thought for a moment. She was trying to remember if she had ever noticed Bob digging anywhere in the short time that he had worked there. The truth was it could be buried anywhere, even off the property. But Vicky had a hunch that Bob would have done anything to keep the spoils from his robbery close to him. He would have wanted to keep an eye on it. He probably knew the whole time that there were criminals searching for it.

Then she remembered the first time she had

realized she made a mistake by hiring Bob. It was when she asked him to finish adding some decking to the employee quarters. He promised it would be an easy task for him, and that he was more than capable of doing it. She had gone out back to check on him, and found him digging beside the deck instead of in front of it where she wanted the deck to be extended. She watched him for a few minutes, trying to figure out just why he would need to dig beside the deck. She was always trying to give him the benefit of the doubt. But then finally, she had asked him.

"Why are you digging over here?" she asked, mystified. "I told you, I want the deck built straight forward from the one that is already there," she reminded him and crossed her arms with irritation. She had even considered that he might have been drinking. She distinctly recalled sniffing for the scent of alcohol, and getting a nose full of dirt kicked by his digging instead.

"I know what I'm doing," Bob had barked at her sharply, as he pushed the shovel back down deeper in the dirt. "Just leave me alone, it'll get it done," he had been very rude and brusque, as if he wanted to get rid of her as quickly as possible.

Vicky had been put off by the way he talked to

her, but at the same time she needed the deck done, so she decided to let it go and walk away. What did she care if he dug extra holes? He obviously was not very bright, and that was something she had remembered about him from high school. He never did very well in his classes. She had never really thought about that day again, since Bob had finished the deck and it had turned out just fine. He filled in the extra hole he had dug, and she had just assumed that he realized his mistake.

"I think I know where he buried it," Vicky whispered, absolutely stunned as the memory played over in her mind. Was it really possible that she had interrupted Bob creating a hiding place for his stolen money? She couldn't believe how naive she had been to think that he was really just looking for a job. She had been rubbing elbows with a violent criminal without even realizing it. He was looking for a place to lay low until he was sure it was safe to spend his fortune.

"Where?" Aunt Ida pressed and grinned eagerly as she snapped her fingers. "I'll get the shovel!"

"By the deck," Vicky nodded slowly, trying to

recall the exact spot where he had dug. "If it's going to be anywhere, it's going to be buried beside that deck!" she said with confidence.

It felt a bit like a wild goose chase. What were the chances that they were right? But what harm would it do to dig a little hole beside the deck? It would do a lot of good if it turned out to be true. They stopped at the garden shed on the way to the employee's quarters to grab a shovel. All of the tools had been inspected and evaluated, but none had shown any evidence of being involved in the crime. When they reached the area beside the deck, Vicky carefully looked over the dirt and grass. She was replaying the memory so that she could find the exact right spot. Aunt Ida couldn't stop talking.

"Oh I bet there are jewels," she said gleefully, her eyes wide and shimmering. "How I love jewels. Just think of all that booty!"

"Aunt Ida," Vicky actually managed a laugh as she began digging where she thought the right spot was. "Bob wasn't a pirate," she pointed out as patiently as she could.

"A pirate, or a thief, what's the difference?" she shrugged mildly with a smile. "Who cares as long as there are diamonds in that treasure chest!" she was practically drooling at the thought.

Vicky thought Aunt Ida's wild ideas were getting a little out of control, but again, she didn't think they would do any harm. As she pushed the shovel deep into the dirt, she hoped there really would be a treasure chest. If there was, she could turn it over to the police, and all of this would be put to rest. Vicky tossed quite a few shovels of dirt to the side. It was hard work on an unusually warm spring day, and she was getting covered in sweat. The physical labor was also aggravating the bump on the back of her head, but she kept digging. Aunt Ida kept prattling on.

"Maybe Bob really did steal it from pirates," Ida pointed out dreamily. "We don't know what he might have stolen. So there really could be diamonds in there. If there is, it wouldn't do any harm to keep just one, now would it Vicky?" she asked with a quiet giggle.

When Vicky didn't answer she looked over at her niece. "Vicky?" she asked again.

Vicky's shovel had struck something hard and

large. Too large to be a pipe. Something was down there under the dirt.

"I think I found it," she murmured back, her brow covered in sweat. She crouched down and began to brush the dirt away with her bare hands. It wasn't long before she uncovered a large box. It was metal, and didn't exactly look like a treasure chest, but it did have a lock on the front that looked like it would fit the small key. Vicky picked it up out of the hole and was about to turn around to show it to Aunt Ida, when they heard a booming voice call out to both of them.

"Put the box down!" Timothy commanded. He was positioned right behind them and must have sneaked up on them while they were busy staring at the box. When Vicky looked up at him she looked down the barrel of a gun that was pointed in her direction. She was terrified, she had never had a real gun pointed at her before. Slowly, with trembling hands, she lowered the box to the ground in front of her.

"Well, I can't tell you both how much I appreciate the two of you doing my dirty work for me," he laughed, and his gratitude actually seemed genuine. Vicky knew why, since the hot day was causing sweat to trickle down her back, and her arms were aching from digging.

"Why don't you just mind your own business?" Aunt Ida snapped, causing Vicky's eyes to go wide.

"Shh!" she hissed at her aunt, who she was certain was going to get them both killed. "Just do what he says!"

Timothy laughed in reaction to the antics of the two and stepped forward to pick up the box. "Thanks again," he called out.

Before he could bend all the way over, Aunt Ida shouted loudly. "Now!"

Vicky only stared as her aunt sprung into action and swung her foot hard between Timothy's legs. Timothy let out a loud yelp of pain and buckled over in pain before slowly tipping to the side and collapsing on the ground. He jerked and curled up, a loud low groan escaping his lips. He didn't look very scary when he was curled up like a baby, with tears slipping past his tightly squeezed lashes.

"Why didn't you help me when I yelled 'now'?" Aunt Ida demanded with irritation as Vicky scooped up the box into her arms. It was a little heavy.

"I didn't think you were going to do that!" Vicky pointed out breathlessly, her heart pounding so hard that she could barely hear her own voice over it. "Come on, hurry up, before he gets up off the ground."

"Oh, he'll be a minute," Aunt Ida said dismissively. "But just to make sure," she landed one more swift kick between his legs just as he had stopped writhing on the ground. Still he clutched to his weapon for dear life.

"I'm going to kill you old woman!" he shouted through gritted teeth and writhed in pain once more.

"Ha, we'll see about that," Aunt Ida smirked and stuck out her tongue at his rude words.

"Let's go, let's go," Vicky tugged at her aunt's hand, there was no time for getting offended by a criminal's words. "Hurry!" She knew that as soon as the man was recovered enough to stand up they would both be in trouble. She thought it would be too much of a risk to try to disarm him, as he was clutching his gun, besides she had never shot one in her life and didn't think it would do her any good to have it. They couldn't run back towards the house, as he was already starting to get up, and to do so would mean that they would have to run past him.

"The truck!" Vicky gasped out as she tugged Aunt Ida towards the staff parking lot. They had a truck for transporting large furniture and loads of supplies for the gardens. Vicky hadn't driven it for quite some time, in fact she was pretty sure that Bob would have been one of the last people to use it. But she still had a key for it on her key chain in case of an emergency or if one of the staff lost the key to it. As they ran across the parking lot towards the truck, Vicky couldn't believe what they had just lived through. She kept glancing over her shoulder to see if Timothy was chasing them. He wasn't. In fact, he had stopped running towards them. He was looking past them when he shouted loudly.

"Get them! They have the box!" Vicky turned back to the parking lot just in time to see Timothy stepping out of his car which he had just parked there. She felt a wave of dizziness as she wondered if she was losing her mind.

"Aunt Ida," she gasped out, thinking that maybe she had a concussion after all. "Are you seeing what I'm seeing?"

Aunt Ida for once was stunned into silence. She too looked between the two men who appeared to be absolutely identical. When she finally found her voice she stumbled over her words.

"There are definitely two of them," Aunt Ida said incredulously. "I just didn't expect they would be carbon copies of each other."

"Twins!" Vicky suddenly cried out as she realized that this was the only way that there could be two of them. That was how one could have an alibi while the other was committing the crime! "Aunt Ida we're going to have to move fast," she hissed at her aunt and pulled her swiftly behind her. If they didn't make it to the truck then it was certain that they would end up just like Bob. Timothy and his twin brother weren't there to play games or to let people go, especially after what Aunt Ida had done to one of the brothers. So their only chance was to get into that truck, hopefully before either of them got off a shot in their direction.

Vicky ran as fast as she could, though she had to be careful not to trip up Aunt Ida at the same time. Still it felt like it took them an eternity to get all the way across the parking lot. The entire time her heartbeats were thumping in time with the sound of the brothers' footsteps digging deep into the gravel parking lot. When she finally felt the cool surface of the door handle of the driver's side door of the truck, she felt an instant sense of relief, as if she had reached home base in a childhood game of tag. But this wasn't home base, and she wasn't automatically safe for reaching the truck. The men were still swiftly approaching them. Vicky tore open the door and pushed Aunt Ida up into the seat. Aunt Ida got stuck climbing over the middle console. Vicky reached up and gave her aunt's behind a firm shove until she tumbled into the passenger seat of the truck.

"Oof, ouch!" Aunt Ida gasped and complained, but it was the only way to get her over the hump.

"I'm sorry, I'm sorry," Vicky mumbled quickly. Then Vicky jumped up into the truck herself. She tossed the box onto the floorboard of the truck on the passenger side and shoved the truck key into the ignition.

"Please have gas, please have gas," she mumbled as she tried to pull the driver's side door shut. Before she could close it all the way, an arm shoved into the truck. It had the same tattoo on the forearm that Bob's did.

"Leave us alone!" Vicky shrieked and slammed the door shut as hard as she could. The man cried out in pain as his arm was crushed by the heavy truck door. In the same moment she threw the truck into gear and slammed on the gas. One of the brothers fell down beside the truck and was half-dragged across part of the parking lot before he was able to get his arm free from the truck. The other brother pulled his gun and was preparing to shoot at the truck, when his identical counterpart commanded him not to.

"Don't! Gunfire will bring the cops, that's the last thing we need! Those two have the box!" he shouted and ran towards the car he had driven into the parking lot. "Hurry up, get in!"

Vicky saw this through the rear view mirror and cursed under her breath. She had hoped that once they got into the truck they would be home free. But the twins were pulling out of the parking lot right behind the truck! Aunt Ida finally managed to get herself upright in the passenger seat. She wasn't hurt, but she was more than a little frazzled.

"Ugh, I think I broke a nail," she fretted as she

looked down at her perfectly manicured fingernails.

"Not now Aunt Ida," Vicky snapped at her, having no patience for her dramatics at the moment, when the situation was already so dramatic. "We have armed criminals chasing after us!"

"Oh I know," Aunt Ida sighed as she looked over her shoulder. "They are persistent aren't they?" Vicky had no idea how her aunt could stay so calm in such a frightening situation, but she guessed it had something to do with her losing her mind.

"Aunt Ida, we are about to die!" Vicky pointed out sharply as she tried to keep the truck on the road. She was driving so fast that it was veering back and forth on the old unpaved road. Luckily for her, she knew the road better than the twin brothers who had never driven on it before. She could maneuver the dips and sudden curves because she had learned to drive on it when she was a girl. Still it wasn't easy to keep ahead of the twins who were in a much newer and faster car than she was. Not to mention the fact that they might decide to start shooting at the truck at any moment. The old truck they were driving in was not known for its reliability either, as Sarah had refused to invest any more money in it. She said they would drive it until it died, and then buy something new. Vicky could only hope that today wouldn't be the day it decided to die.

"That's it!" Vicky suddenly declared. "I'm not going to risk my life without even knowing what's in that box!" she fished the key out of her bra once more and handed it over to Aunt Ida. "Open it up, let's at least see what's inside before these crazy brothers run us right off the road!"

Aunt Ida reached down to the floorboard for the truck and grabbed the box. She settled it into her lap and then tried to slide the key inside the hole. It was no easy task because the truck was bumping and bouncing up and down all over the road. Finally she got the key into the hole and turned it. Vicky glanced over briefly as Aunt Ida opened the lid on the box. They both gasped with surprise. The box was stacked high with what appeared to be hundred dollar bills. There had to be close to a million dollars inside of it.

"That's a lot of money!" Vicky gasped and tried to keep the truck on the road. "No wonder they're chasing after it so fiercely!"

"Hmm." Aunt Ida mumbled as if she was entirely unimpressed. She was rummaging through the stacks of cash. Finally she sat back with disappointment. "I don't think that there are any diamonds in there," she frowned.

"With that much money you could buy plenty of diamonds!" Vicky announced, though her attention was more focused on the car that was gaining on them fast. "Aunt Ida hold on!" she called out as she turned the wheel on the truck hard to the right. She knew of a small side road that she was sure the twins wouldn't know about. The truck listed hard as if it might tip over, but it finally settled back on all four wheels. She glanced over at Aunt Ida to be sure she was not hurt, but the woman was just looking through the money again.

"Maybe we could just take a little," Aunt Ida suggested as she began slipping some of the stacks of money into the deep pockets of her jacket.

"Aunt Ida," Vicky growled as she glared at the older woman. "You put that back in the box right now. That's stolen money, it doesn't belong to us any more than it belonged to Bob and his acquaintances. Put it back!" she insisted with a ferocious tone. She didn't usually speak to her aunt in such a way, but she was at the end of her rope.

Aunt Ida let out a loud and dramatic sigh. "I thought you were the fun one Vicky. I'd expect Sarah to make me put it back, but you?" she looked very disappointed.

"In the box!" Vicky snapped, she didn't have time to be more diplomatic as the twins' car had negotiated the turn onto the road right behind them.

"Can you please try calling Mitchell, or the sheriff," Vicky said desperately, she knew there was no real way to escape the twins. "We're going to need some help or we're never getting out of this," she tossed her phone to Aunt Ida who caught it easily. She busied herself with the phone, cleverly forgetting to put the money back into the box. Vicky gunned the engine and reached the end of the side road. She pulled out onto a larger paved road that still saw very little traffic.

"Hello?" Aunt Ida shouted into the phone. She wasn't the most knowledgeable when it came to technology. Sarah and Vicky had tried to talk her into using a cell phone, but Aunt Ida flat out refused. She called it a leash, and said she was a free spirit who couldn't be collared.

"You have to hit the green button Aunt Ida," Vicky explained to her as patiently as she could. In her rear view mirror she saw something sticking out of the passenger side window of the twins' car.

"I hate these newfangled things," Aunt Ida complained as she shouted into the phone again. "Hello? Hello is there anyone there?" she shook the phone with annoyance. "This thing is broken, I'm sure it is!"

"Get down!" Vicky shouted and pushed her aunt down in the seat, using her free arm to shield her head and neck. "They're going to shoot!" She did her best to duck as she braced herself for the gunfire. "Keep your head down!" she commanded, fear creeping into her high pitched voice.

Chapter Five

Mitchell looked down at his phone as it began to ring again. It was Vicky's number again. He glanced up at the sheriff who was studying a map of the area around the inn.

"There's so many little roads back there," he sighed as he shook his head. "They could be hiding out anywhere, really," he paused a moment to look over the map again.

"So where would the killer have gone?" he was musing to himself, and getting nowhere fast. Mitchell had waited long enough. He wasn't going to let Vicky think he was ignoring her if she needed his help. He snatched the phone up off of the desk.

"Don't you answer that phone Deputy," the sheriff warned as he spun around to face Mitchell. Mitchell openly defied him as he lifted the phone to his ear, and met the eyes of his superior.

"It's my job to make sure she's safe," he said flatly, as if it was no longer open for debate.

"Hello? Vicky?" he asked quickly. Then he held the phone away from his ear as he heard someone shout.

"Get down, they're going to shoot!"

"Vicky?" he shouted into the phone, his voice full of alarm. "Are you there? Where are you? Who's shooting at you?" he was desperate for information.

That got the sheriff's attention. He marched over to Mitchell and began listening in on the conversation. Finally a voice came back on the line.

"Hello is this Mitchell?" Aunt Ida asked, sounding very confused and aggravated.

"Yes, I'm here," Mitchell said quickly, relieved to hear that she wasn't terrified. "Where are you? Is Vicky with you?" he fired off his questions swiftly.

"Tell him about the twins," Mitchell heard Vicky call out in the background. "They need to know there are two!"

"Listen Mitchell, do you remember that good looking young fellow Timothy?" Aunt Ida asked as if they were settling into some beauty shop gossip.

"Yes, Ida, are you safe? Where are you?" he asked more firmly this time. He could tell something terrible was happening but the woman on the phone was acting as if everything was fine.

"Well, as it turns out there are two of them, twins," Ida laughed into the phone. "Isn't that amazing?"

"Tell him we're near the inn!" Vicky shouted desperately. "We need help, Mitchell!" She couldn't drive and talk on the phone at the same time but Aunt Ida was taking things too lightly.

"They're near the inn," Mitchell told Sheriff McDonnell who immediately began to radio for cars.

"Are you in danger?" Mitchell asked as he ran out of the police station and towards his cruiser. There was no way he wasn't going to get as close as possible to them. "What's happening right now?"

"Vicky is driving like a lunatic," Aunt Ida explained calmly. "But that's only because one of those boys is pointing a gun out of his car window at us!"

"I need a location," Mitchell said desperately as he started his cruiser and began driving in the direction of the inn. He was definitely not obeying the speed limit.

"Well, I can't really say where we are, we're driving so fast," Aunt Ida attempted to explain as the truck bumped over some patches in the road.

"Can you get back to the inn?" Mitchell asked hopefully, it was the one place he knew that they could find in the myriad of dirt roads and roads that weren't even identified on the map. "We have cars going out there right now. If you can get back to the inn then you'll have some help," his voice was trembling as he felt he was too far away to be of any real help.

"We can try!" Aunt Ida replied and then turned to Vicky. "He wants us to get back to the inn, he said police are on their way to help us," now her voice was shaking slightly, as if the danger of the situation was just beginning to set in.

So far the twins had not taken a shot at the truck, but Vicky knew that if they evaded them much longer they would. The truck would not serve as any kind of shield from the bullets and the twins were not likely to give up. After all with the amount of money they were after they certainly wouldn't care about two more murders.

Vicky turned hard to catch the street that would lead them back to the inn. Luckily the twins missed the turn and Vicky was able to get some distance between them. She had the gas pedal to the floor when the engine began to sputter. The old truck was about ready to give out. She could see the inn in the distance rising up against the mid-morning sky. Never before in her life had she been so desperate to get to it. She took a deep breath and tried to calm her nerves. Now would not be the time to lose control of the truck.

"We're heading that way," she called into the phone that her Aunt held up for her to speak into. "So far they're not shooting, but they are definitely armed."

Meanwhile, the sheriff was running the information they had on Timothy. It was sketchy at best, but when run with the new information of Timothy having a twin brother, they came up with a match. In fact, it was an identical match of a man who was Bob's cell mate. A man who had been charged in the past with crimes related to murder for hire. The sheriff was being driven by one of the rookie officers to the inn when he got on the radio to all cars available.

"We are dealing with some very dangerous individuals, who are reported to be armed. Please proceed with extreme caution, and remember we have civilians in the middle of all this, so be careful what you are shooting at!" He then looked over at the rookie officer and barked at him, "can't you drive any faster?"

As Vicky drew closer to the inn she could see the flashing lights of police cars against its stoic walls. She felt a slight sense of relief, but that relief disappeared when the twins' car began ramming them from behind. They must have seen the flashing lights as well and were trying their hardest to run the truck off the road before it could reach the inn.

"Aunt Ida we're going to crash," Vicky warned, her voice shaking as she spoke. "I can't keep the truck on the road much longer!"

Just then she heard the squeal of tires and the sound of gunshots. She closed her eyes briefly, expecting to feel the pain of a bullet at any moment, but when she opened them she was still pulling into the long driveway that led up to the inn. The twins' car was no longer ramming them from behind. She dared a look in the rear view mirror and saw that a police cruiser had pulled up behind the twins' vehicle and taken out both of its back tires. The car had spun off into the ditch beside the driveway. The driver of the cruiser emerged with his gun drawn.

"It's Mitchell!" she cried out with relief as the truck sputtered into the parking lot of the inn before finally giving out. The truck was immediately surrounded by police cars that were waiting for them. Officers jumped out to escort the two women from the truck.

"He needs back up!" Vicky announced with desperation in her voice, but other cars had already driven up behind Mitchell's, including Sheriff McDonnell's. Several officers were pointing their weapons at the twins' car. The two men began climbing out of the car as Vicky and Aunt Ida were whisked to safety within the inn's walls by two police officers.

"What a ride!" Aunt Ida cried out with glee as she peered out the front window to see what was happening. Vicky was anxiously watching to see if Mitchell was safe.

She watched as the twins surrendered their weapons to the officers and then lay down in the driveway to be cuffed. They knew there was no way to get out of the situation now. As soon as Vicky was sure they were in custody she rushed out of the inn. Aunt Ida followed right after her.

"Do you have any idea how much danger the two of you were in?" Sheriff McDonnell demanded as soon as the two brothers were escorted away to a waiting police cruiser. All of the officers were now congregated in the parking lot of the inn.

"Of course we do," Aunt Ida said as she furrowed one perfectly thin eyebrow. "We were there you know. I bet you don't even know that youngster threatened to kill me, and," she gasped and lowered her voice, "he called me an old lady!" She pursed her lips and tilted her chin upward, then cast her gaze towards the sheriff as if she was a fashion model. "Now, do I look old to you Sheriff McDonnell?" she asked.

The sheriff looked a little flustered to have her attention lavished on him in such a way. "Ah well, no, you don't Ida, not at all. Just as beautiful as you've always been, I have to say," his ruddy cheeks grew redder with blush as he glanced away. Despite the fact that Vicky had just been through one of the most terrifying experiences of her life, she couldn't help but smile at her Aunt's antics. She was the ultimate flirt, and could charm any man that set eyes on her.

"Vicky!" Mitchell came running up to her and without thought to the fact that Sheriff McDonnell was watching him, he threw his arms around her waist and drew her close to him. "Are you okay? Are you hurt?" he stared so deeply into her eyes that Vicky was more than a little taken back.

"I'm fine," she assured him as her heart fluttered slightly and she began to feel comforted by his muscular arms around her. "Thanks to you, of course."

"I'm sorry," he said, suddenly recalling his role as a deputy sheriff. He reluctantly released her and stepped away with an apologetic frown. "I should have answered when you called, I wish I would have, and then maybe none of this would have happened."

"That was my fault," Sheriff McDonnell said sternly. "I ordered him not to answer the phone because I thought you would distract him."

Vicky narrowed her eyes at the sheriff. Although he was finally there when they needed him, she still wasn't a fan.

"Well maybe instead of being so worried about how distracting I might be, you should have paid closer attention to what a fantastic deputy sheriff you have," she said sternly. "If it wasn't for him finally answering the phone, Aunt Ida and I would probably still be in big trouble."

Sheriff McDonnell nodded remorsefully. He stopped short of apologizing, but the look in his eyes showed he knew that he had made a mistake.

"He is a very fine deputy," he admitted with a hint of pride in his voice. "Do you two have any idea what these two men were after?" he asked darkly.

"No!" Aunt Ida whistled as she tucked her hands into the pockets of her jacket to hide the money she still had stashed there.

"Yes," Vicky countered, offering her aunt a scathing glare. "Aunt Ida, we have to tell them the truth."

Ida scowled, but nodded in agreement.

"There's a box in the truck," Vicky explained with a sigh. "We dug it up from the garden. Inside I believe you will find the missing money from whatever crime Bob committed."

"It turns out Bob was a cell mate of one of the twins," the sheriff replied as some of the officers went to the truck to begin inspecting the box and its contents. "That is why he had the same tattoo as Bob. It's a prison tattoo. Only one twin has it."

"Ma'am, could you please empty your pockets," one of the officers asked Aunt Ida in the most respectful tone he could muster.

Aunt Ida sighed and nodded reluctantly. "I was just keeping it safe," she smiled sweetly as she handed over the stacks of money to the officers.

Vicky smiled affectionately as she shook her head at her Aunt. She also watched to make sure all of the stacks of money were returned.

"You two were amazing," Mitchell said with genuine astonishment. "You cracked the case. If it were not for you, we might never have caught these two, and they could be off living on the stolen money."

"No, they were not amazing," the sheriff corrected with a fierce scowl. "There's nothing amazing about putting their lives on the line and interfering with police work."

Aunt Ida rolled her eyes and gave the sheriff a light pat on his bicep. "Now Sheriff, it's okay that you didn't figure it out, it was a very complicated case after all. Who would have guessed twins?"

The sheriff was not appeased by her words in any way, and patted the handcuffs on his belt lightly.

"Next time you two pull a stunt like this, I'll make sure you're in handcuffs," he warned with such a damning glare, that Vicky did not doubt that he meant every word.

"Next time?" Vicky gasped and shook her head firmly. "Hopefully there won't be a next time!"

Sheriff McDonnell cracked a smile at Vicky's words. "Now that this case is solved, I hope that things will go back to normal around here. I'm a little too old for all this action!"

"Not me!" Aunt Ida declared as she laughed and hugged Vicky around her neck. "I had the time of my life!"

Sarah pulled into the driveway just in time to see the police cruiser with the two criminals in it drive away.

"What in the world happened here?" she asked as she rushed up to her sister and aunt. "Is everyone okay?"

"It's a very long story," Vicky sighed as she smiled at Mitchell. "But the important thing is that we're all safe, and the inn should be free from police soon, right?"

Mitchell glanced at the sheriff for an answer.

He frowned. "We'll need to do a final collection of evidence, but that should be done by this afternoon. So I suppose we can be out of your hair by tomorrow."

Vicky sighed with relief. Even though she had just gone through a terrifying experience, the bride who was waiting to have the most wonderful day of her life, was still on her mind. She couldn't wait to make the call that would let her know that her wedding was in the clear. As she dialed the number Aunt Ida was busy filling in all the details for Sarah.

"In a hail of bullets, I'm telling you, this one was driving like a fiend!" Aunt Ida exaggerated as she slipped her arm through Sarah's. Sarah glanced with concern in Vicky's direction but Vicky only shook her head.

"They never actually fired at us Sarah, we're okay. It's all going to be fine now." Just then the bride answered the phone. "Yes Jennifer, I just wanted to let you know that everything is still on for this weekend. Don't worry, there won't be any sign of police presence, everything will be perfect," she assured her. When she hung up the phone her smile had faded.

"What's wrong, did she cancel?" Mitchell asked her as he stood beside her.

"No, but I do have a bit of a problem," she said as she glanced at him.

"What is it?" he asked as if he would bend over backwards to do anything to help her.

"She's invited me to be a guest at the wedding, I just don't have a date," she cleared her throat slightly.

"I like weddings," Mitchell volunteered and arched an eyebrow. "Unless you'd rather take Henry."

Vicky laughed at that idea. It felt good to laugh after so much tension.

"Then Mitchell, will you be my date this Saturday?" she asked.

"Yes I will," he replied and slid an arm around her waist. "I would be honored."

Chapter Six

The garden looked beautiful. In addition to all of the colorful blossoms that lined the long, cobblestone pathway, there were carefully tied ribbons in the pale rose shade that the bride had chosen to match her bridesmaids' dresses. The sky was a pure and clear blue, as if it was ready to celebrate the day right along with the multitude of guests that were attending. The lush, green property around the inn was once more pristine and magical. There was no sign of the police tape that had roped off the garden just a few days before.

Vicky had been very careful to make sure that there was no evidence left behind, no memory of the terrible event that had taken place. She had even hired a new gardener to come in and make sure that the weeds were cleared and the numerous plants had been nourished as best as they could be. Even though a part of her still regretted hiring Bob in the first place, she felt a special sense of gratitude that she had been able to help solve his murder. She still believed that no matter what crimes Bob had committed he shouldn't have had to die in such a traumatic way.

Vicky was adorned in a simple burgundy dress that draped from a roman neck to a loose sweep against the cobblestone. Aunt Ida had helped her to select the garment. Sarah had stood by, offering her votes of approval on both the dress and the up do that Vicky's brown locks had been pinned into. Her deep green eyes seemed to match perfectly with the rich hues of the garden that surrounded her. As stunning as she looked, Vicky still felt a little nervous about seeing Mitchell again. They had called and texted a few times since he had come to her rescue, but she still had to wonder if it had all been just a day on the job for him. She couldn't deny that something new was stirring within her, a desire for Mitchell to want to spend more time with her. It was something she hadn't expected, and had just come out of the blue.

"You look amazing," a voice said from just behind her. Vicky turned around with a slow smile as she recognized the voice.

"Thank you Mitchell," she replied as she drank in the sight of him in a dark blue suit. She rarely had the chance to see him out of uniform, and he was even more handsome in her opinion.

"Thanks for inviting me," he said with a murmur as he stepped up beside her. "Everything looks beautiful."

He wasn't looking at the garden. His striking, blue eyes were gazing directly into hers.

"Shall we?" he asked and offered her his arm. Vicky wrapped her arm around his and they walked towards the wedding staging area. All of the white chairs were set up in even rows with an aisle covered in rose petals between them. Vicky was sure the bride would be pleased as the petals were almost the exact shade as the ribbons she had chosen. Vicky loved attending to the little details of a wedding. It was delightful to know that she could bring someone's dream to life and provide them with the beautiful experience that they hoped for.

"I can't believe you did all this yourself," Mitchell said with admiration as he sat down beside her in the back row of chairs.

"Well, I had some help," Vicky admitted as she winked at Aunt Ida who was flirting heavily with one of the violinists. Though the violinist was at least twenty years her junior he seemed enamored by the woman's charm. Then she glanced at the watch on her wrist and waved him off to do his job.

Aunt Ida joined Vicky and Mitchell in the back row, eager to see the bride make her entrance. As the violin music swelled through the air, Vicky saw Jennifer in her snow white gown. She looked just as she had hoped, joyful and full of anticipation. It might have taken a lot to make sure her special day remained special, but Vicky was glad that she had made the effort. It was a moment of pure happiness that Jennifer and her new husband would never forget.

"No matter what may have happened here," Vicky murmured to Mitchell as the bride glided past them, "all of the bad memories will disappear, and all of the wonderful memories will remain forever."

The End

More Cozy Mysteries by Cindy Bell

Hairspray and Homicide (A Bekki the
Beautician Cozy Mystery 1)

A Dyed Blonde and a Dead Body (Bekki the
Beautician Cozy Mystery 2)

Mascara and Murder (Bekki the Beautician
Cozy Mystery 3)

Pageant and Poison (Bekki the Beautician
Cozy Mystery 4)

Made in the USA
Middletown, DE
18 July 2022

69658217R00076